Autumn
in the
Abyss

D1595668

Autumn in the Abyss

By

John Claude Smith

Omnium Gatherum
Los Angeles

Autumn in the Abyss
Copyright © 2014 John Claude Smith
"Broken Teacup" first published
in *Grave Demand Magazine* 2012

ISBN-13: 978-0615972732
ISBN-10: 061597273X

All rights reserved. No part of this book may be reproduced or trans-
mitted in any form or by any electronic or mechanical means, including
photocopying, recording or by any information storage and retrieval
system, without the written permission of the author and publisher.

http://omniumgatherumedia.com

This book is a work of fiction. Names, characters, places, and incidents either are the products of the author's imagination or are used
fictitiously, and any resemblance to actual events or persons, living
or dead, is entirely coincidental.

First Edition

For Alessandra and Gabriel, two whose presence in my life is a source of constant inspiration.

"After one look at this planet any visitor from outer space would say 'I want to see the manager.'"

—William S. Burroughs

Table of Contents

Autumn in the Abyss 9

Broken Teacup 54

La mia immortalità 71

Becoming Human 84

Where the Light Won't Find You 112

Autumn in the Abyss

"The Word is a living thing."
—Marco Cinque, poet.

From Rene Zimmerman, author of *Listening to the Voices: A Compendium of Explorative Literature's Forgotten Masters* (Unsafe Harbor Press, 2009):

> Visionary poet Henry Coronado's 1956 beige Ford Fairlane was found abandoned, aslant off the always scorching strip of asphalt designated as California State Route 127, shadowing the southeastern edge of Death Valley, early July, 1960. Nobody knows how long it had been there. Nobody knows what happened to him. His final statement to the world was more concrete than poetic: the driver side door was left open.

He was gone, never to be heard from again.

Though there seemed a surfeit of suicides and mysterious deaths and disappearances within the literary community during the '60s and '70s, in particular the concentrated realm of poetry and experimental fiction, I cannot attest as to why Henry Coronado's story so fascinates me. Of all those who passed, his fame seemed flimsy at best, with nothing to substantiate it beyond recollections by those who knew him and his sparse poetry. No complete works remain, only piecemeal stanzas and sentences which vary in construction and confirmation among those who claim to have known his work. He's as much rumor as fact, a phantom shuffling between question mark and ellipses.

Poets didn't get famous unless they were blunt forces of nature like Charles Bukowski, or so truly gifted their work endured the test of time like Pablo Neruda, Dylan Thomas, and Walt Whitman. Coronado was Bukowski without the alcohol and rage, without the unflinching glare on the reality of squalor and grit. His words portended a reality just to the left of ours, more fantastical but conveyed in a way no less blunt, no less honest, than Bukowski's. Or so those in the know alleged. Coronado saw the world with different eyes, as Beat writer, Jack Kerouac, had noted in one of his last interviews, a drunken ramble that never made it to publication. In my research, I was able to obtain a copy of the disjointed transcript, almost an abstract prose poem in and of itself. Kerouac seemed more disillusioned than usual, more drunk as well, yet a sober knot tightened as he expressed his admiration for Coronado's work, saying, "it had ...more truth, more guts in his taut lines than anything any of us would even admit to having seen, witnessed, experienced. What Coronado wrote dug deep into the psychological landscape of America. He saw the '50s split in half, a battle forged between nuclear threat and the eroding American dream. A piss-stained white picket fence. He saw the ideals inspired by these ideas as the monsters they truly were. Monsters of the mind, the id, ego and neurosis made real. This was compounded and magnified by his general distaste for the human race, something that rubbed many in the Beat community wrong. Though, of course, he had nothing to do with Beat poetry. It was just bad timing on his part to have lived and made his smudged mark during the genesis of the Beats."

What I didn't understand until listening to a CD burned from the original reel-to-reel recording of the Kerouac interview, and hearing it in his voice, was the monsters of the mind were in no way metaphorical. There was stress in his voice, tension, the pace of his conversation shifting down, conspiratorial. I would say that leant more credence to his interpretation of Coronado's standing in the poetry world. He believed Coronado was a keen observer of the real world, of reality and didn't have inhibitions about stating exactly what he saw. My take on what Kerouac seemed afraid to divulge— perhaps having as keen an eye as Coronado, but being less inclined to embrace what he truly saw, despite his own works that embraced a freedom, a lifestyle, outside of the norm— seemed eerily prescient when he muttered toward the end of the tape, something not included on the transcript of the interview, "But he was right, you know? Coronado not only confronted these monsters, his demons, he brought them into play with his words. I thought they weren't *real*. Coronado proved I was wrong. I don't know how much more I can take, how much knowledge any human can take."

Kerouac was dead three months after the interview, perhaps as much from his alcoholism as the years of knowing whatever it was he really knew. Perhaps his alcoholism was a direct result of knowing too much.

You may wonder how I got the transcript, and, more so, the recording, if the interview was never published, and Martin Gayles, the interviewer, died in a one car accident the same week as Kerouac— another mysterious death left unexplained. The accident happened during the late afternoon on the Santa Monica Freeway. No drugs or drink were noted in the autopsy.

Some mysteries shall remain mysteries even to me, much like my shut in tendencies. When I started my research, claiming it was for a biography about Coronado,

I contacted Sherrie Gayles, Martin's wife, about the rumor of the Kerouac interview. She denied it existed, rather forcefully for a woman of eighty-four years old. According to the nurse at Rolling Hills Senior Living she was "...wallowing deep in the throes of dementia." The nurse seemed doubtful Mrs. Gayles would be of any good to me, yet mention of that interview seemed to give the old woman focus, clearing the confusion of her thoughts and improving her memory.

"Best to leave it be, sir. Best to let the demons sleep. Best to let them sleep forever."

With her speaking of demons, I felt the nurses might be correct, and she was well beyond reliable: she was outright mad. Yet, when I hung up, I sensed something more awry. Her tone, her inflection, was much in line with Kerouac's cracking voice during his final statements on the recording.

It was as if I had reminded her of something she never wanted to think of again in this life or any that may follow.

~

A large envelope with my name and address written in firm block letters was dropped through my mail slot a week later. With no return address.

I called Rolling Hills Senior Living to talk to Mrs. Gayles, only to find she'd passed away the night after I had called. The slim possibility she'd sent me the burned CD was gone. Unless, of course, she'd made calls to somebody else about my query but... none of this made sense. She had adamantly stated there were no remaining recordings of the interview.

I left it to the Gods and carried on, my research uncovering even more Molotov cocktails disguised as chewy chocolate bon mots.

A week after receiving the envelope, another smaller

envelope slid through the mail slot, dropping as a secret whispered in a willing ear. I heard its muffled plop as I was responding to an email to Roberta Bline who had worked at USC with Coronado for the two semesters he had lasted in 1954, before he left in a huff because his teachings were deemed incompetent. Bline had hinted that his methods would be considered progressive nowadays. The hushed sound shook me from my concentration. I made way to the door and the lone letter, picked it up and noted it had no stamp. It had not been delivered by the postman, as if I got anything but junk mail anyway. I opened the door and anxiously scanned the unkempt yard, the decrepit houses that surrounded me. The weary world outside.

My agoraphobia kicked into high gear. I yelled out a feeble, "Hello," to no avail. The street was as dead as my freedom. Sweat poured profusely down my face, pooled in the armpits of my threadbare gray polo shirt. I closed the door and let out a weighted sigh, a release that magnified my forlorn condition. My heart was beating so loudly I knew another minute or even handful of seconds might send me to the floor, never to rise again.

After regaining some element of composure, I looked at the blocky lettering, not unlike what had been on the envelope with the transcript and burned CD, and realized it was not even addressed directly to me. My name was not on it at all, yet the message written across the sealed yet empty envelope read: *Do you really want to take this path?* My discomfort boiled in my belly or possibly deeper. Butterflies grew thick, leathery wings and fluttered madly there. I desperately wanted to run outside and hail the messenger for questioning, yet the thought of even opening the door again made me woozy.

My struggle for composure demanded rest. I slumped on the sofa, on the side where the springs had yet to eat through the fabric.

Upon awakening, I found the day had grown cold and dark as best I could see through the slits at the sides of the always closed curtains. The shadows snuggled into the furniture and unlit hallways. I turned on a lamp that flickered— as if undecided as to its purpose, bring light or surrender to the dark— before steadying itself.

"Yes, I need to take this path," I said out loud. "I need to know what happened to Henry Coronado."

My voice was weak as my Cowardly Lion's courage, no matter the determination it articulated. My obsession won out, though acid bubbled enthusiastically at my esophagus. Something large scampered across the roof, paws pounding the slate shingles, crushing them into shards; pummeling them as if attempting to break into my house by sheer force of intent.

I stared up at the ceiling, at the always present shadows that shielded the stippled landscape just below where the commotion centered, for what seemed like hours. I was detached from myself, detached from living, until the more concentrated rattle and hum of the many clocks that filled the walls, cluttered tables and even my wrist— the metal band seemed melded to my flesh, a symbiotic embrace: a cruel reminder of all the time lived, wasted, leaving a snail trail as it passes— forced me to check the time. My watch read 1:43; a.m. or p.m., I did not know. As if it mattered— I snapped out of my stupor, my concentration regained, and headed to the den, ready for more research.

> While we were into experiencing everything, a tactile wonder, the kiss of stars, the only two poems I read of his [Coronado's] reeked of pessimism and a hatred of his fellow man. We were into freedom of expression. Drugs and drink and orgies abounded. I was quite

pleased Coronado never made it to any of our orgies. [laughing] That's why it always struck me as odd that he connected so strongly with fantasy artist, Russell Randlebot.

—Diana Voorhees, poet.

Many who had taken the time to respond to my correspondence had suggested getting in touch with Russell Randlebot would be the most fruitful venture for gathering anything of substance for my biography, though none of them had a legitimate phone number, email or snail mail address. Most claimed Randlebot had an aversion to phones, making the possibility of him even having a computer less viable.

Late '50s minor experimental fiction phenom, Dora Sallee's response even aligned itself to the strange envelope message/warning I'd received a month earlier, stating in her brief email: "Are you sure you want to do this, Mr. Smith? Some things should remain mysteries. You dig too deep, you may find something you really don't want to know." Her curt response was not unfamiliar as most of my feedback had been brief at best, but her coda made the butterflies wings thicken again, reminding me that Coronado was not a popular subject and that, really, it might be best to leave it be. Yet, after all these years, I needed to know the truth, having boxed myself in this house and letting curiosity fester as a wound, a scab forever picked at, never healing. This was a mystery worthy of facing head on.

Of course, contacting Randlebot might be the detour that led me away from finding anything of substance when it came to Coronado's disappearance because his self-imposed exile since 1960 has made him almost impossible to find.

Almost.

As my diligent research turned from hours and days into weeks, it revealed the shocking fact that Russell Randlebot not only lived in this same desolate town, but only a few blocks down the street!

This discovery sent me to my bedroom for days, blankets pulled to my neck and often over my head when the sounds on the roof grew in intensity. The terrible din suggested the horrors of animals being disemboweled. The ever concentrated pounding, as if the force of desire would create a door in which whatever animal was up there— it seemed much larger than a cat— would barge in and carry on with its vicious ways upon my flabby belly, feeding, feasting, gorging... The startling, improbable truth of Randlebot's whereabouts bolstered my agoraphobia into a full on panic attack, inspiring fevers that baked my cranial cauldron. My brain, stirred and fueled by a sense of dread so palpable I could feel its bitter joy burn in the back of my throat, could intuit the beast's malignant companionship as it wrapped me in its glacial embrace.

Because the only way I could get any information from Randlebot would be to step outside my house, this self-imposed prison constructed by my wayward brain, wardens Paranoia and Trepidation mangling my every thought, and walk the few blocks down my street to his house.

And knock on the door.

My groceries were delivered once a week from the local Safeway. I would slide the charge card through the mail slot and nervously wait for the charge slip to sign and for the delivery person's footsteps to fade away. I would wait longer than necessary before forging the strength to open the door and scramble in and out, hoisting the paper bags into the entranceway, because opening the door, taking in the stale, often frigid air from outside, filled me with a panic I did not want to face. Ever.

Besides these few occasions to open the door, my life was lived in this tiny, crestfallen house, disrepair its dominant quality. The foundation was encrusted with rust that coated pipes, nuts and bolts. I scrubbed the black mold out of the tub whenever motivation gripped me to take a shower. Furniture unworthy of junk yards cluttered the tiny rooms. The refrigerator groaned and wheedled all night. Dishes bred in the sink. Filthy palm prints stained the urine yellow walls— signs of balance attained in my weakest moments. The musky stink of old sweat, layer upon layer of the stench, flooded my nostrils. Shadows never left the ceiling. All hidden corners harbored empty memories.

It had been this way for as long as I could remember.

Soon after I'd discovered Randlebot amazingly lived a mere few blocks down the street from me— it might as well have been another city, another country, perhaps Mars— I received another sealed-envelope: *Quietly fade away, "Mr. Smith," and let it be. Nothing is worth the knowledge you seek.*

All I wanted was to know what had happened to Henry Coronado. Why was this veiled in secrecy? Who was wary of my trespass?

Quotation marks around my name also suggested the message writer knew of my charade. I had chosen Mr. Smith as a generic pseudonym for my research, not wanting anyone to pry too deeply into my history, to intrude on my already physically and mentally crowded space. One must do what one must do to dig for answers. After years of uncertainty, I needed answers.

I wondered if Russell Randlebot had heard of my inquiries through the literary grapevine. Perhaps an old friend still in contact with him, one I had gotten in touch with, had relayed the information.

Perhaps he was sending me these messages, yet it all

seemed incomprehensible. Agoraphobia breeds paranoia, one's mind always enveloped in one's thoughts without distraction. The only way to know would be via action. Stepping out the front door, walking along that desolate street, and saying hello to Randlebot in the flesh.

> We had gone beyond a point of no return, and we were ready for it. None of us wanted to go back to the gray, chill, militaristic silence, to the intellective void— to the land without poetry— to the land of spiritual drabness. We wanted to make it new and we wanted to invent it and the process of it as we went into it. We wanted voice and we wanted vision.
>
> —Michael McClure, poet, at the Six Poets at Six Gallery event, after Allen Ginsberg had read "Howl" for the first time.

"Russell Randlebot and Henry Coronado met in San Francisco at the famous *Six Poets at Sixth Gallery* reading, October 7, 1955. This was a landmark event for the ferocity with which one poet, Allen Ginsberg, launched his salvo, "Howl," onto the unsuspecting packed room. The crowd included a drunk Jack Kerouac who stamped his empty wine jug shouting "Go!" punctuating each line with enthusiasm and fervor. An Event had taken place. Amidst the wild camaraderie and the drunken revelry, Randlebot recognized a sullen Coronado with a smirk on his face. He was the only member of the audience not embracing the universal euphoria. Introducing himself, he helped shake Coronado from his odd malaise, drinking too much vodka in the process. Randlebot and Coronado woke the following morning in the narrow alley next to soon to be famous

Beat bar, Vesuvio. They carried on much of the following day engaged in conversation, dreams, and drink."

Immersed in Abraham Kalinski's posthumously published *The Beats Out Beyond* (City Lights, 1961), an historical tome on the world of poetry in the '40s and '50s— he'd passed away from "natural causes" New Year's day 1960, during the hullabaloo outside of The Camera's Eye nightclub in San Francisco, California, where Henry Coronado had just had his first and last reading— I was in my head, taking in the magic, the madness, the madmen and mad women who gave themselves up to words. The polished vision was broken as I heard what had to be my third missive from the mysterious messenger drop to the floor beneath the mail slot.

Actually, I had not heard it, but sensed it. I went to the door and there it was— another message. This one was scribbled on a torn piece of paper, as if no sealed envelope was deemed necessary, that familiar block lettering etched hard into the paper, with but one word: *Stop.*

I crumbled the paper in my fist, a comedic show of defiance. Me, a man afraid to step outdoors.

I knew where this was all leading. I would have to find the will, the strength within, to battle my demons and whatever demons lurked outside my door, and talk with one enigma— Randlebot— to acquire insight into another enigma— Coronado— to appease the niggling obsession that had taken roost in my brain. A worm eating to the core of an already rotten apple.

As was habit for me, though, I allowed the worm to leisurely feast. Anything to delay the inevitable.

I read more from Kalinski's tome, of Coronado and Randlebot's intense, fiery relationship. Randlebot had been married, though the parameters of marriage meant nothing to him as his promiscuous nature had led to many affairs. Upon connecting with Coronado, his marriage dissolved. As witnessed in public, Randlebot's affections had approached idolatry. Coronado, though, expressed himself as he always had, still adorned with a mask of aloof impudence—"a real condescending bastard, don't know how Randlebot could deal with him," poet Peter Orlofsky had noted. But a handful of times Randlebot seemed to regain his self-respect and lit into Coronado with rage and fisticuffs to boot. Yet always, within a day or two, they would be spotted together again, deep in conversation, as if nothing had happened.

Kalinski's book had been published in 1961, a little over a year after his death. A little over a year after the infamous (and quite prophetic) 1959 *New Year's Eve Welcoming Chaos* reading at the now defunct The Camera's Eye nightclub in San Francisco's North Beach, a haven for the Beats. Though Coronado was in no way a Beat poet, simply being a poet in San Francisco in the '50s meant acknowledging the classic venues of the Beats, such as Caffe Trieste, Vesuvio, City Lights Bookstore, and the aforementioned The Camera's Eye, as well as poets and writers and artists imbued with the outsider mindset.

Moving on to Kimberlee Caspian's slim, *Coronado's Pandemonium* (Stagnant Vertigo, 1972), I got a more succinct overview of the defining incident in Henry Coronado's life and a harrowing occasion for those who experienced it firsthand.

The Camera's Eye *Welcoming Chaos* event featured many visionary poets. Their poems were less Beat-driven and more wide-eyed and terror-filled. Philip Lamantia debuted a series of interconnected poems, "The Stars in Our Souls," that featured cosmic imagery of a scintillating nature, yet he abandoned the purity of this path because of the incidents that followed the event. Grant Marlock and Sharon DeVries also exhibited exemplary work of

depth and vision that left the audience awestruck, especially DeVries with her scatological rant, "My Gender is
a Weapon," which had nothing on the outside to do with
gender issues. It was more an excursion through the
underbelly of life in the city as perceived by an unknown,
perhaps alien, entity. It was chaos to the nth, the perfect
lead in to Coronado's first and last reading.

Though Coronado had been a force within poetry circles
for a decade, he'd had no books published, had performed
at no readings. A smattering of poems in small press jour-
nals had been the extent of his output, yet these vital, bleak
poems had left a huge impact. His reticence had kept him
out of the limelight until Randlebot had convinced him to
do the New Year's Eve reading.

After Lamantia, Marlock, and DeVries had read, the
place had reached a fever pitch. Coronado took the stage
at 11:45 p.m. with the intention of reading three poems—
two of his highly-praised published poems, and a new one
written especially for the occasion, what Randlebot called,
"an epic piece in style, scope and hallucinatory vision, a
bridge between now and our unmapped future." The poem
was introduced as "Autumn in the Abyss," yet confirmation of the title was immediately in question. Lamantia
claimed Randlebot had told him the title was "Coronado's
Pandemonium" (hence, Caspian's lifting of it for her book
about the event), while other attendees suggested variations of both.

Not that any of this mattered. As Coronado took to the
stage surrounded by candlelight and incense, he quickly
read his first two poems to moderate applause. The residue
of DeVries manic reading had yet to dissipate. Coronado's
feeble, anxious reading, his voice cracking, his eyes skit-
tish, was "severely putting a cramp on the evening," as one
patron put it. "One would think a man of his formidable

stature would have a voice worthy of God, but he showed no signs of being able to live up to his swiftly dimming legend."

Before his reputation was completely ruined he returned the focus to himself in a curious way. He walked around the stage and snuffed out the candles set in stylish, wrap-around wrought-iron dragon sconces along the back wall, then stepped out to the front row of the audience and did the same to the candles in matching dragon candle-holders on the tiny tables. He pinched each wick as one would do to oneself in a particularly bad dream, praying for escape.

There was no true escape from what followed.

Coronado was almost fully immersed in darkness. The dim light from the remaining candles on the table tops behind the front row cast brooding shadows that danced in a macabre fashion in his direction. Some witnesses spoke of shadows without a foundation in reality, figures lurking and looming, as if culled from the stone walls. His presence gained a foreboding aspect, his countenance etched with an eerie quality most described as frightening. The papers he'd read from during the first two poems were scattered to the floor. He leaned into the mic and recited in a voice many claimed was much different than the insecure timbres he'd adopted during the first two rushed readings— as if this one was the only one that mattered—"My gift for you, all of you who disgust me deeply, is true pandemonium. Dark revelations with apocalyptic consequences. Only I understand what the mere speaking of these words will bring, though you will taste their venomous intent soon enough." At this point, an anonymous member of the audience blurted a disparaging, "Evil, man," much to the shushing chagrin of others in attendance. Coronado's strange transformation sobered up all but the most soused. His mouth stretched wide, "the leer of a sated hyena," according to poet Neal Cassidy, and continued: "Chaos is the god of logic, the only god worthy of humanity's misguided meanderings. The logic of madness. The madness of true pandemonium."

Silence from the audience as he paused, sobriety snuffing out even the most slippery tongue.

"And He speaks through me."

After which, reports conflict— even the confirmation of the exact words he spoke. Each person questioned for the book, as well as by the police, said something different. Some took this version— the most succinct piecing together of his words— and changed it into something that suggested monsters of the id and ego. Others agreed with Kerouac's curious, post-interview comments that suggested the corporeal existence of monsters *outside* of the id and ego. Everyone knew one thing: two dozen people died that night, a dozen in the fire that engulfed the venue, another dozen in accidents and suicides in the few hours past midnight.

Perhaps most troubling of all was that three of the suicides killed themselves by mutilating their eyes. Burgeoning poet, Marianne M plucked her eyes completely out of their sockets with a spoon.

Furthermore, no one could confirm anything beyond the introduction to the poem, yet there was, as with all recollections from the evening, enough evidence of "lost time" to suggest a mass hallucinogenic experience. Authorities suggested that drinks may have been tampered with, spiked with a drug of immense potency. Reports had Coronado starting his reading of the final poem between 11:50 and 11:52 p.m.. The bedlam hit full force just after midnight.

As I read these recollections, dicey as they were, a sense of dread escalated within me, much as when my agoraphobia becomes overwhelming. I felt Coronado's presence within me, a flickering light of recognition, and felt the weight of his words. These strange feelings were born of those words, I was sure. I scribbled incoherently, blocky letters like toppled skyscrapers, yet I could not put those words to paper. My unease escalated. Nausea swam as sharks around a raft, blood from the injured staining the water, increasing the menace, their hunger. Yet my obsession remained resolute, no matter my discouraging physical reaction.

I owned Kalinski's tome, a pricey acquisition via eBay many years ago, but Caspian's book— a footnote in Zimmerman's comprehensive appendix— was nowhere to be found. Even evidence of her publisher, Stagnant Vertigo, was non-existent. When I was about to give up my search, I lucked into finding a website with the complete text— something that did not take any special keywords to access, just the umpteenth typing of variations of the title, author and publisher, yet one last time— and there it was. I would say it was the fitting reward for my hard work, yet the reward seemed more a curse as the night enveloped me. It was a thorn in the paw of my obsession as there was no contact info for Caspian, the publisher, or even who-ever had set up the website. All info was nil beyond the text from the book.

The wind rattled my house with such might as to inspire a thought to skip through my mind of The Wizard of Oz and Dorothy's tornado-inspired trip. My agora-phobia swelled. The confines of my house seeming more claustrophobic than welcoming. Sweat beaded and raced down my thick jowls. Showers being a rare commodity— my girth and apathy or simply pathetic ways inspiring minimal quests for hygiene— my already pungent aroma grew moist lending a moldy, maggoty taint to the already repulsive stench, ambience... life. No wonder my inclina-tion was to stay inside this rat-trap abode. My sour smell and sour mind were content to pollute only within these already tainted walls, not intruding on the stale air and stale landscape outside. As if it mattered.

As if on cue, the roof became a playground for incomparable chaos— a different source of chaos than at Coronado's first and last reading, yet I felt a connection, an impossible bridge between the two disparate events— as what sounded like a dozen large animals trampled the already splintered shingles, their intent on feasting on whatever crossed their path, or perhaps battle for supremacy. They were kings of the world above and outside mine. Screeching, mewling protests, iron-willed howls, wire-brush scratching and sonorous laments echoed in the bones of my jaw. My teeth chattered. My wherewithal was withdrawn.

Or perhaps it was God pounding on the roof— wake up! Wake up!

I palmed a fistful of aspirin into my mouth, chewing and swallowing with determination, as if aspirin could stop the anarchy above me. I knew it couldn't— the anarchy loomed always, waiting for my guard to waver— but at least it might derail the oncoming migraine. I pushed away from the computer desk, the creaking computer chair relieved at my exit, wrapped my stained white terrycloth robe tighter around myself and covered up the evidence of my loathsome being. I had to regain my focus, move it away from myself, as nothing there was ever of worth, and back to Coronado, a man of questionable worth and much mystery.

But as the commotion continued on the roof, I waddled back to my bedroom and covered myself in shabby blankets, stuffed my sausage-thick fingers into my aching ears. A useless shield against the world outside and my hellish existence in here.

Hours or days passed, I did not know. The many clocks that clattered as a convention of cane wielding men, an unrelenting *click, click, click* sounding like distant gunfire, or perhaps far enough to be cannons, with a cannonball about to bulldoze my house, tear a hole through the front door, open me to the mercy of what lay beyond— *dear God, please, no!*— meant nothing to me. Nothing, other than where the mind takes it. My perversely persuasive mind; my perversely *perverse* mind...

I peeled the blankets off. My robe was drenched with the sweat of sleep spent in nightmare landscapes. It was always like this, every awakening confirmation of the legitimacy of Misery and Disgust.

I made my way to the kitchen on wobbly legs, the firecracking joints in my knees and hips in need of oiling. When I pulled on the handle of the refrigerator, the suction seemed stronger than usual. I wondered when I'd last opened it. I spied dozens of crumpled ramen packages on the sticky countertop— eaten raw as all of my pans were either passing time with the filthy plates and glasses in the sink, or crammed into every nook, cranny, or shadowy corner within the refrigerator incubating whatever repellant leftovers that filled them. As the door opened with the sound of a forced kiss, these thoughts and the foul smells that wafted from within— alien and indescribable— impelled me to slam it shut. I would not be eating anything from in there. I clumsily tore the cellophane off a carton of ramen and snatched three bags before heading for the den.

Settling into my computer chair with a grunt as it groaned, I tapped on the mouse and a murky light radiated weakly from the monitor. Tearing into the ramen package with my teeth, I squeezed out a mouthful of the hard noodles and took a bite.

Coronado's "Autumn in the Abyss" according to those in attendance who were still able to comprehend what they had experienced dwelled within each of us. It was a paradoxical seed rooted within spirituality that some perceived as the heart of his atheism, while others considered it an extension of his early use of opiates. Although Coronado claimed he stopped years before, to 'keep his mind sharp for the forthcoming battle.' From what others have pieced together though, his so-called visionary lines had deteriorated into pure fantasy. Unreal, but not surreal. He hinted at other beings, perhaps Gods, which as far as I cared, invalidated the gist of his new work. He wasn't forecasting the future in his ever fatalistic manner. He was imagining the unimaginable, which might work for horror fiction, but as poetry of substance, no. Sorry. I don't get it and I don't care. Nobody's been able to paste together a precise version of "Autumn..." anyway.

—Carlos Dragonfly, poet.

Coronado feigned ignorance and even malice as to the depth of the tragedy that had transpired that evening. "Perhaps the truth is a bit too ruthless for the masses to experience. No matter how open-minded they claim to be. It's not up to me to limit perceptions, to put a stranglehold on reality. It's up to me to open doors. It's up to me to show the way. It's up to others to decide whether to step through those doors." The use of the word *ruthless* really set my teeth on edge, rubbed me in a way I found unnerving— an enthusiastic sandpaper massage of naked flesh— yet also forced me to reconsider my understanding of my obsession. I wondered if the darkness he trumpeted with such contempt for his fellow man was the source of my attraction to him, not just his strange disappearance and the rumors that hounded him. Was I simply ogling the accident out of human curiosity for something, some-one, so ugly? Really, what drove me to *need* to know more about this human stain? His attitude repulsed me, yet his attitude was shaped much as mine was, as mine is now, by my distrust of all that is human.

My confusion simmered, needling me with the thought that my obsession had more to do with envy than abhorrence.

I laughed out loud— a choking insult to the act. Chewed noodles sprayed on my keyboard. Something shuffled slowly on the roof as if being dragged.

With the tragedy of the *Welcoming Chaos* event, since much of the crowd had imbibed enough alcohol to make any three port-bound Navy crews envious, the quality of the information was less than stellar. Outsiders looked at the tragedy with snide deprecation as if they thought it the product of a misguided movement, jumbling the event within that negligible branch of the arts the Beats occupied, even if it had nothing to do with Beat poetry, per se. Online reports were limited at best. The only note on the fire was that it was started by "carelessness." Nothing more. Strangely enough, there was nothing to be gleaned from the online archives for newspapers from that era, either.

Russell Randlebot went into seclusion.

He had suggested the event, had even worked with the owners of the venue to promote it. After the deluge, the madness and disorder, the deaths, he wanted nothing to do with poetry, art, or Coronado. His only comment on the event, before taking on his hermit existence and living off the money his paintings and art books had garnered: "I was excited about where it was all going. We were all excited about where it was going. But Henry... I prompted him to leave certain esoteric elements out of his work. He simply shrugged his shoulders as if none of it really mattered. But I knew it mattered. He lied to me before the event, saying he would not mess with the really dark stuff. That was his way, though. He was a real manipulator. Then he took it too far. It was an abomination he unleashed." When asked to explain his last statement, according to the interviewer— Candace McClean, a hot shot New York critic for the arts, —Randlebot stared at her with a sorrow she expressed as "palpable," yet his response was curt, filled with a simmering rage: "You're an idiot if you want to dig deeper, Candace. It's all of our deaths you'll be hastening."

Again, the oblique nature of Coronado's existence rose to the top, cream to be skimmed off and fed to his demons, his legend.

Over the next decade, conversation, analysis, and dissection of "Autumn in the Abyss" reached a fever pitch as it dominated the poetry world. Candace McClean's 1977 article for Art News, *Autumn is the Winter of our Discontent*, pieced together a dozen stanzas of the poem gleaned from the fractured reports of survivors of Coronado's reading. In mapping out stanzas from the poem— yet not the complete poem, an utterly impossible task made more evident with her article— a curious disassociation seemed at odds with her goal. The lines had a mutable quality, ever-shifting within the landscape of memory. Evolving to fit the mindset of the individual. McClean posited the ninth stanza portended "atavistic yearnings that emanate from deep within." According to her, the stanza opened with the line, "My bones glimmer luminous beneath saltwater flesh," which perhaps aligned itself with her interpretation, if one was immersed in a fantasy mindset.

Poet, Jack Harolds, described the stanza as "a vital

stream-of-consciousness examination of the worth of humanity in the budding age of peace and love as saddled with aggression and self-satisfaction," while famous under-ground self-proclaimed "word-slinger," Albert Albert, suggested it was "that moment of final choice or perhaps recognition, the 'dying dreams of corporate allegiance' he wields as an ax, to chop down what remains of the *good old days*." Bukowski called it the "no-holds barred truth," which might make Coronado smile, if he were still with us.

None of these examples— and there were dozens more— even hinted at McClean's "atavistic yearnings" take on it. Of course, the three poets mentioned above hadn't even been at the event. Was their understanding of the noted stanza culled from McClean's take on it? Of course, to each his own, and within the academic, ego stroke world of poetry, over-thinking the words of others was common. Yet for me, as I read the ninth stanza on a website, *the words didn't even match up!*

"My bones glimmer luminous beneath saltwater flesh?" She stated in the article this was the opening line of the ninth stanza, yet at the end of the piece, when she gathered together the shards she had collected, it was not present. McClean, usually a meticulous researcher, built one entire section of her argument on this example, yet on the final page, where a mere twelve stanzas from her own recollec-tion are posted, there was no indication of its validity.

The ninth stanza I read from the online archives for *Art News* opened with "Venom as the root of the sleep-ing yet not dead language," might also align itself to some sort of atavistic yearning, yet what of Albert Albert's take and his inclusion of his reading of the line, the words— "dying dreams of corporate allegiance"—within his response? What were each of them reading? Why, with McClean's reputation, has she floundered so badly here? Bukowski's statement even caused me to laugh out loud.

"No holds-barred truth?"

My confusion rose. "Turbulence embroidered on flesh, tattoos painting husks with the conspiracies of the soul." My thoughts acclimated to the poem, yet researching the line— *I know I have just read it on my monitor, the article was there, still there*— it was nowhere to be found.

My confusion solidified. I was wary of much more of this, yet my obsession needed finality.

McClean briefly touched on Coronado's disappearance, a cursory account. Nothing to hold on to. Nothing more.

The words were all Coronado had truly left us. Primarily, this incomplete poem. This incomplete poem with its contradictory lines.

It was clear my research had reached an apex. It was clear that the only path left, the avoided path, the dread-filled path, was to head out to Randlebot's house.

Time was inconsequential to the agoraphobic. I was an unmoored being: drifting, drifting...

No mirror in my bathroom— no mirrors in the house— made my hygienic task a blind exercise. It did not really matter. I showered and shaved, brushed my teeth with an always empty toothbrush. I dressed in charcoal slacks and an off-white shirt; it used to be white, but the years fed on the purity and left it faded, yellowed, much as I expect my teeth to be. I was compelled to slip my dress jacket over my bulk, but my prodigious size inspired sweat and no matter the temperature outside. I left the jacket behind.

Smudged reflections glanced back at me from the metallic skin of the toaster. Faces from a gathering crowd. Faces whose features cut through with expressions of clarity: a pale woman with white hair and a feline smile; an old Asian man with almond eyes that spoke of secret knowledge; a young Latino girl whose innocence was history. I swiftly turned to avoid scrutiny. They suggested something hideous, but confirmation was against my true interest. I knew already what a mirror would reveal, what resided inside: this soiled soul.

I thought for a moment about the last time anybody had seen me in the flesh. My recollection turned to dust. It had been years, perhaps a decade or two, three.

I was stricken with a shade of melancholy as I could not even recall my age. Memories extended arm's length. That was all. My mother, father, any siblings— all resided in a windowless room in the back of my brain. The door was locked, all access denied.

My disgust boiled. Worse yet, now that I was ready to leave the house, to wander along the desolate streets of this austere avenue, I was hesitant. I was afraid. Not so much for what Randlebot might reveal, but of the air outside so different from the familiar musty smells of which I was accustomed. Of the possibility of people out there, watching me, perhaps even one or two who might ask of me... anything.

I screamed, a foreign utterance. The primary voice I've heard for years has been the one in my head. This aural intrusion was a blasphemy to anything remotely human. I was embarrassed. I was revolted. My very being trembled at the thoughts, the possibilities. My breath grew rapid, my heart thumbing a ride with it. Everything grew hazy, my head lightened— a balloon escaping to freedom in the center of a powder blue sky while the child cried at the loss— and, overwhelmed, I fainted.

What must have been hours passed, my bloated body festering as a fresh lesion on the never vacuumed green carpet. Awakening, I pushed myself, with much effort, to a sitting position. Motes of dust shuddered above me. The lone lamp's dim rays spotlighted them as they floated and scattered.

I stood, using the ramshackle sofa as a crutch, and took in the disaster that was me. My shirt was soaked through.

My slacks as well— perhaps I urinated on myself, though the smells indicate sweat, but with such a malodorous abode, I could have been wrong. The part of me that never rests took over— my always buzzing, whirring, warring mind with gears grinding incessantly spat thoughts out in random patterns. It spewed my own internal poetry, perhaps as vital as any poets' words that had ever come before. I almost smiled at such nonsense. This momentary levity served as inspiration, as distraction, and I cared not at all as I waddled toward the front door, reached out with the rare steady hand for the cold door handle, turned it, and swung the door open.

Dusk or dawn, I'd no idea. It was an in between time, which seemed appropriate. I was in between, always in between. The moments in between were my fondest friends. Allies in this self-made hell.

My first step out the door was a lifetime in the making. I vomited on the porch, my reward for such courage. Or foolishness. I was aghast but followed with another step, this one perhaps only decades in attainment. As I took these broad strokes, the details came into focus; my focus, perhaps the only thing to keep me moving forward during this gruesome charade. If anybody was watching me, they must have been laughing at the fat man's stuttering dance. Perhaps calling friends, all their friends, Come, watch the comedy of errors. Come ogle the forlorn freak.

But then, the reality became clear. The sky was darkening, so dusk won out. The street was even more desolate than the weekly awkward dragging of grocery bags into my home would attest. A mere few steps out the door and I was astonished by the barren, besmirched vista before me. The few cars in front of decrepit houses suggested Negligence or perhaps Abandonment as their only riders now. The dreams of motivation, of speed, long since faded. Lawns littered with weeds, some that towered as tall as me, provided perfect hiding places for my neighbors, those laughing at me now. Shuttered windows at least suggested they might not even care to venture outside to get their fill of the fat man's rare appearance.

I wondered how I originally had come to this drab, indistinct neighborhood. Had it materialized out of thin air, a product of my buzzing, whirring, warring brain?

My own yard, from this perspective, tottering on the cracked walkway from my door to the curb, bloomed with weeds so diseased as to cause my stomach to roil. Plump heads on thick stalks caused the spines of the stem to droop unappealingly. I thought of a convention of hunchbacks all huddled in grim conference. Bereft of petals, the illusion of beauty was left unfulfilled. The skin was mottled and a pale green liquid leaked out, dripped to the dirt, fed the plants, and this horrible cycle rolled on and on, multiplying ugliness with every generation.

What a dreary place to live. No wonder everybody stayed inside as I did. Who would want to step out into such a bleak world?

I had a flashing thought to turn and visually explore the roof, to see the remains of whatever mad revelry was often played out there, but the curiosity was slaughtered by the thought of one, two... a dozen of whatever animal it was that reigned there staring down at me, a hearty feast for their insatiable appetite. I made sure not to look, avoiding their glare for fear of ending up down their gullets, just another meal in the long line of meals that fill the instinctual needs but not their ravenous tendencies, forgotten upon ingestion, a constant loop. Just like my day-to-day existence.

I carried on my sluggish trek, my legs aching already as I passed by my fourth house. My already drenched shirt stuck to my flab as wind joined the oncoming night. The chill, though, was almost invigorating. Something different, this experience. Had I ever experienced this before?

Minutes shriveled as lazy moths bounded again and again off the occasional functioning street lamp, something that did not light my way, so much as show me the moths' kamikaze surrender to *their* obsession. The urgent tapping rhythm of insect bodies bouncing off glass, begging entrance into the land of the enlightened, mocked the hesitant pace of my quest. I snicker inside at this thought, though outside, no laughter escapes, not wanting to hear the rusted gargle of my voice. A few of the lucky ones attain their goal, sizzling as they hug the hot glass, an end to their ludicrous routine. I lift my eyes to watch their victory, distracted from my fractured path. Diverted from a sidewalk overtaken from beneath by thick roots and an array of weeds punching through with vigor, or lackadaisical impetus, or simply a stronger desire to live than anything else in this cheerless neighborhood. Though it must be noted, my path was also littered with pockets of the pale green liquid as it seemed the trees were infected much as the weeds. Infected, such a strong, negative word. Why must I think of everything in this depressing way? Perhaps the pale green liquid was simply their lifeblood... toxic and spreading to infect everything.

I could not change the way I thought, my mind the toxic elixir upon which I slake my analytical thirst.

The night was deep and unforgiving. Hours passed as I squinted to read the numbers posted on the fronts of houses steeped deep in disrepair. I finally spotted Randelbot's address. His house seemed on par with mine, on par with this miserable neighborhood. This sickly street littered with disease and so hopeless, so hopeless...

I questioned myself about carrying on. If I could carry on. If I had the courage. After all, conversation was not my specialty. The hacking sounds recently scraped from within are evidence of this. Yet why submit myself to such torture without at least knocking? I hoped that nobody would answer so I could run as fast as my aching legs would take me, to home, to hell, to my private hell. To obsessions that would not let me go until they compelled me to make this trek again— *dear God, no*. The thought forced bile to scale my gullet, yet it simply burned, unreleased.

The night was darker than one would imagine, the wind lashing with intent— warning or whipping me for my folly?— as I made my way to the door. My sweaty, meaty fingers gathered as a fist. My knock was feeble, weak, an extension of my desire to be gone.

Praying for no response…

…as the doorknob turned and the wood groaned, the jamb squealed, and the door opened slightly. An invitation?

I mustered the wherewithal to say, "H-hello," in a tiny voice, the voice of the insignificant. A rat scratching at a wall.

There was no response. But I sensed a presence near. One perhaps as sullen as me, trapped in his own private hell. After all, if Randlebot had been in seclusion since 1960, it was quite possible he was my equal in the pitiable throes of agoraphobia. Then again, if he was, who slipped the messages to me? If he made that trek three times— I could not imagine such determination.

I angled my face toward the space between the outside and the inside, and took in the familiar smells— smells I knew! Smells like my house. We *were* of the same wretched ilk, the fabric of our existence as grubby on the outside as the inside.

I said, this time louder and, dare I say, firmer, "Hello."

Still no response, yet there was a hint of an echo, one ridged in sighs. My momentary flagrant association with courage grown brittle, I knew I had only one choice at this point, one option.

I needed to step inside, away from the wind and dark,

away from the outside, the ever oppressive outside. I relished the opportunity to shut out the world, but in another's house, the comfort passed as a dime-sized kidney stone.

I closed my eyes and pushed the door open, took three quick steps, stopped, slammed the door behind me. I opened my eyes, expecting to see Randlebot, an aged Randlebot, his once handsome features— a chin sculpted from the sheered white cliffs of Dover, majestic blue eyes the envy of Maxfield Parrish's paintbrush— devoured by time. What I saw instead knocked me to my knees.

I emitted a moan of defeat as I took it all in. As I took in my house, my furniture, my smells. *My hell.*

I took it in as tears welled and flowed, undammed. Overwhelmed.

Laughter, a grumbling, uncontested and evil laughter, shook me to the core. A dark, wet blossom bloomed on my slacks. My heart's rhythm thundered within my heavy, sagging chest, seeking escape, refuge— anything to invalidate what burned my irises as my pupils expanded. I swear I could hear the sizzle...

"Hello," said a voice etched out of spite and wicked contempt. A sinister voice riding the tail of the grumbling laughter.

"Randlebot?" I said, uncertain only because this was my house, my hell, no matter my trek.

"Randlebot, Randlerot," the voice said, a snicker in the intonation. Cruelty personified. The dagger thrust in with force and gleefully scraped bone.

The answer suggested nothing and everything, confusion at its core, the ever magnificent and ever vile chaos that rules the labyrinthine mind reeling at the possibilities.

"Your pathetic condition sullies the night sky with its plumes of black-winged bewilderment blotting out the stars." The wood cracked and settled above me, an exhalation courted by exhaustion.

"I don't know what you are suggesting, Randlebot—"

"Randlebot, Randlerot, Randleriddles are all you've got."

The seed of frustration bore diseased fruit. "If you are not Randlebot, then who are you? Who the hell are you?"

"You were warned from the beginning not to disclose what you discovered. But you liked to push. You liked to toy with humans because you felt they were beneath you. You were warned but heeded not the admonishment." The heat of his presence was a bloody, freshly skinned bear pelt wrapped around my quivering girth.

And the words he littered as bread crumbs along the path to contrary truths made no sense to me. Warned? What I had discovered? What *had* I discovered? Was this a reference to the notes dropped in my mail slot?

"I needed answers, despite your so-called warnings. My mind allows no respite until answers are attained. It's a curse of my obsessive nature, as well as my pathetic condition, as you call it, and I do not disagree."

A tripwire snapping at my casual trespass: "You still have no clue. We spoke of warnings long ago, when you were young and still able to imagine freely. When your imagination explored too deeply, yet we allowed your trespass... under special circumstances, yet you ignored even those."

I was at a loss. A rag doll shaken in the mouth of a rabid Rottweiler. My head light, as if punctured and losing focus: "What are you talking about? What warnings if not the notes dropped through my mail slot." And, as the question turned from mist to cement in my head: "Who are *we*? If not Randlebot, who are *you*? *We*? What the hell is going on?"

My nerves twitched as a thousand shit-coated flies rubbed their insect legs together, cleaning off the filth before indulging in more.

"You won't like the answers."

You might regret the intrusion. You might regret your existence—"

"To hell with your condescending manner." I leaned forward, head lighter still, as if emptying all its contents. I tried to catch myself on the arm of the sofa as I slumped to the puke, green carpeted floor. Dust motes took flight, a momentary escape from the drudgery of non-existence. "I need to know all there is to know about Henry Coronado." Suicidal? An obstinate child?

"Good," he said, they said— the voice enunciated— stretching the single syllable word into something monstrous, a python's embrace.

I attempted to situate myself on the sofa, pulling at the arm, but my body was weak and clammy, already beaten. What more could their revelations and verbal flagellation do? Yet, I needed to see it through.

"Randlebot, Randlerot, our liaison, was sent to keep you on your path of discovery. Full disclosure was to be our gift to you, but not something to share. He was sent to keep you in check and failed. "

"Sent to me? Sent to me when? From his hiding place down the street from me or...?"

They ignored me. The inflection of their blatant fiction boring even to them, as if they had better things to do than pass time with me. I did not blame them. Yet, they continued.

"'Autumn in the Abyss' was never meant for public consumption. Randlebot, Randlerot had attempted to keep you from reading it at the Welcoming Chaos event, raving over your other potent, but less persuasive piece, 'Coronado's Pandemonium.' But you in your ever—"

"Stop with the references to me as Coronado," I said, my voice cracking as old crust. I struggled as my head filled with flashing images that rolled out memories that could not be mine. The implication of their words influenced my thoughts, or perhaps altered them, much as a hallucinogen could.

Again, ignoring my plea— give me truths, damn it, not these impossible fictions— they persisted: "You in your ever vigilant hatred of your fellow humans chose to unveil the darkest words ever. Not purely because of *content*, but because of *intent*. This sequence of words was loaded, explosive, apocalyptic."

Dear God! I wondered as to their madness and for once felt strong, better than somebody else. My contemptible existence was perhaps not the most contemptible existence this world had ever witnessed. These people, this undefined *we*, these voices from the shadows, never revealing themselves this indefatigable storyteller crushed to gruel under my large feet and swallowed by the shadows it called home might be a more worthy possessor of the disgraceful crown.

"You tire me, Randlebot, Randlerot or whoever you are. Show yourself or leave me to my meager existence. I may be repugnant, but you don't even rate that unworthy distinction. Be gone." I waved my hand, a plump pigeon taking flight.

"Even after years of isolation, you still find the *cojones* to treat someone you think of as human and inferior with such brazen disdain." They found the capacity to laugh— a coarse cough, a stern bleat—which really riled me.

"Be gone or be seen, wretched one. Or the wretched many. Then leave me be. You've no information of worth. I have to get back to my real research and chalk this up as time wasted."

Shuffling sounds, something moving in the back room, my bedroom, the bathroom. Perhaps this puny intruder was looking to escape through a window. Perhaps—

"As you wish." Their voice echoed from the bathroom, a refrain that lingered too long, as if calling to me, insistent.

"Come forth without any more games or stories. I've had enough," I said, rising from the floor. Patting the dust off my pants, as if the action mustered merit when, really, the pants were already soiled. But I gained a sense of faux vitality in the process. A strange illusion, one of many to come.

"'Mirrors and copulation are abominable, since they both multiply the numbers of man'" Quoting Borges seemed irrelevant, until I sensed the undercurrent of unease upon which the quote was founded. *My unease.* A nod to impossible disclosures.

The bathroom with its bland wallpaper— water color blue gulls of no real distinction— and its stained porcelain, its slow leaking faucet, and the prevalent black mold coating the caulk between tiles of the shower, was the ambient manifestation of my *genius loci.*

I sensed the obvious lie within the statement, within Borges' words. The only mirror in this house had splintered into a shower of shards under my heavy fist what seemed eons ago. Why should the voice suggest something as ridiculous as the possibility of a mirror when there isn't one in that shoebox sized room? Why should the thought of my reflection, after all these years, make me recoil inside, my intestines squeezed tight as sleeping rattlesnakes?

Rattlesnakes awakened and moving to the meat of my heart, the muscle flaccid from years of inattention.

Nothing made sense. This mad day was one to shove aside and forget, like all the rest of the mad days which, in retrospect, can only be viewed as insipidly normal days. All the rest of the days strung together as notches on a noose.

I made the hallway in silence, except for the sloth-like dragging of my feet on the pockmarked carpet, worn to the hardwood floor beneath by thousands of tramps along this path, yet all I wanted was to avoid this one, but for the pull... the pull...

Truths of this nature, they come on rare occasion in our lives. Facing them, perhaps we grow, gain a glimmer of wisdom. Move forward. Unless you are like me. The thought of facing anything outside of my dull parameters caused the rattlesnakes in my belly already craving my heart to beeline toward the head, my brain. Perhaps it would be a sweet mercy, their gorging.

Nausea wrapped me in its sweaty fist squeezing vertigo from my head and bile from my stomach. My throat constricted blocking the uprising. Some squirted through, scorching my tongue, varnishing it in the vestiges of my escalating fear.

Yet still, I moved forward or, rather, was being pulled, pulled...

...when I made it to the closed door.

A snigger of malicious joy, satisfaction escaped from within the bathroom. The smudged metal door handle rattled as I reached to open it. I hesitated, my trepidation omnipresent as a mule kick to my head. I felt faint again, yet braced myself on the wall, not wanting to touch the door.

My agoraphobia was a profound thing, more viscerally present *right now* than when I had walked outside— if I had actually made that trek as the evidence seemed negligible. I suffered because of the voice of the many or the one, mumbling incoherently from beyond a simple bathroom door, one I'd opened thousands of times.

I reached for the door handle again, my heart pounding in my ears, pounding so loud I expected it to either leap out of my chest as a marlin on a taut fishing line, or simply stop in the presence of such breathtaking fright and drop me as a sack of shit to the floor. Food for insects and rats, only to be discovered years later, stripped to the bone.

Unknown. Never Known.

As my fingers greased the knob, it continued its rattling, sodium-vapor shock, cockroach dance beneath them. I closed my eyes, turned it... and pushed.

I stepped forward and into the room. The dank smell cut by the crisp, bitter taint of urine caked on filthy porcelain assailed my nostrils and brushed as a chilly breeze across my sweat-coated face.

I opened my eyes to stark truths, absurd epiphanies, madness... chaos! Impossible lies...

I found myself seated on a vast, cooling desert floor, all that empty space cloying, stifling. I hiccupped and vomit spilled out of my trembling lips, staining my shirt. I glanced down at myself, leaner yet still large. Confusion reigned. Yes, the implications were clear, yet the sense was lost on me.

I was Henry Coronado.

But I *was not* Henry Coronado. *I couldn't be.*

I shivered as the night crowded in on me, an invisible horde pressing against my chilling body.

With my eyes I followed a scorpion until it scampered beyond my view and a figure ambled from its retreat. Were they one and the same? I watched the figure as it approached grow from fitting into my palm so I could easily crush it, to standing above me, looking down with a familiar face.

He pulled a handkerchief from his back pocket. His clothes, a dark suit, were indistinct, yet that face...

"Jack Kerouac? Jack Kerouac?" My voice sounded different, more clear, yet still in need of tuning, as if scanning a radio dial for the perfect intonations or the proper timbres.

He ignored my cries, my obvious surprise. His always intense eyes, an inner knowing threaded around the pupils suffusing them with fatalistic understanding— at least as seen in the photos and YouTube clips I'd watched— stared down at me, though his expression was one I could not read.

"Wipe yourself off, Henry," he said as he handed me a monogrammed white handkerchief with magenta trim.

I took it from his pale fingers, neon pulsing from the phalanges. I wiped and did not hand it back to him, because of my revulsion for those glowing bones and tossed it aside. It sparked and transformed into a couple dozen mutant flies, preposterous and huge, extra eyes, extra wings. They puffed tiny cigars as they lit into the darkness, circled the moon, then radiated in swift flashes of light, shooting stars: make a wish.

I wished I was anywhere but here.

Kerouac lit a cigarette butt, a bloated thing. In the light from the match and his shimmering fingers, I saw movement beneath its lipstick-stained skin.

"If I pinch myself, will I wake up?" A stupid question; an inane plea. Kerouac only smiled.

"Sure, not that you'll wake to a life of different circumstances. Just back to the same old, same old, Henry." A wry smile, knowing. "Limbo in the land of Nod. You've been asleep for years, Rip Van. Your somnambulant existence was courtesy of your swelling ego and of the power of words you so flagrantly flaunted, man. You knew too much and decided to share. This, my friend, was your downfall, setting you on this unenviable path, Henry—"

"I am not Henry Coronado!"

"Believe what you want, Henry"—a smirk laced with scorn and a trace of sympathy— "but you are who you are, though in reality, in the world outside of the world you know so well, Henry Coronado fades a little more every day. Soon, maybe a decade down the line, you will be nothing more than rumor. A minor player in some fantasist's repertoire. A blip. Or nothing. A never was, not even imagined." He sucked on the cigarette and held it for the briefest moment, before exhaling a plume of mutant flies, relatives to those I had witnessed a mere minute or two ago. Though these whispered as they flew by my ears. Language, words... I heard their tiny chattering *voices*, nonsense ribbings of Henry Coronado. Of me.

The light pulsing from within Kerouac's fingers shimmered neon white and purifying.

Facing one's true self, denial no longer an option, can be an illuminating experience, if one understands the hows and whys of such a long denial, of such a dreary existence. My eyes welled but no tears spilled. Rivers left dry; dreams never remembered. Never dreamed.

"You see, Henry, way back then, you were warned, man, you were warned." He took a deep swig from a large jug of wine I hadn't noticed yet. Expected, perhaps, but hadn't noticed. "Oh, thanks, Henry. I much prefer the drink to, well... almost anything, at this point."

Resigned, I said, "Carry on," my inflection rooted in a cold, calm defeat. A cold-blooded confirmation as the skin on my arms rippled as scales. A snake in need of a morsel; a morsel of information. A morsel of diamond hard truth.

"Coming 'round, eh?" A forked tongue flicked between his cracked black teeth. "Some people, not even specifically creative sorts, purposefully or more often randomly, push the limits beyond a point that we deem acceptable. It's dangerous."

"What's dangerous? Succumbing to the allure of one's muse—"

"Muse," he said, a mocking amusement caressing the utterance. "I suppose getting to the gist is paramount to cutting away the fat." He shook his head. "Muse has nothing to do with what *we* are, my friend."

The universal "we" again, him and the voices in his head or perhaps the others, the unseen participants in this cruel game.

He slapped his hand to my back. Not out of friendship, but out of condescending ire. "We enjoy speaking these things, letting ourselves roll out and the beauty of us. We are woven into the fabric of it all, man. Of everything. We are the common ground even if delivery is unfamiliar from one person to another. Ground zero. The thrust of alpha and ejaculation of omega." His eyes went glassy. He seemed to relish the image, the words. "We participate at all times, even in silence. The ever screaming silence within your head and all those who breathe through the desperation and futility that dominates the earth."

Words collided in my head, brakeless cars converging on a freeway with no exits, no way out... and all leading to the same central destination: the gist, as he called it. I mentally flailed on the freeway, hands tied behind my back, blindfolded, the car motivated by a volition all its own. I was simply along for the ride.

I broke the spell, this senseless meandering through the clutter within my head and asked, "Who are you? Not you, Jack. But the *we* you speak of?"

He looked at me aghast, a clown with his make-up removed, the illusion blown. "'I am large, I contain multitudes.'" Quoting Whitman as a dodge; then again, perhaps the truth was something I failed to consider. He continued, clarification or more obfuscation: "Why, Henry... *We* are words. The key aspect laced into every person's life."

"Words? What do you mean, words? I don't understand."

Kerouac harrumphed, annoyed, and took another seemingly endless swig from the bottomless jug of wine.

"We are words, Henry. More so, we are the intrinsic aspect of words. We are that element that keeps them alive. Words are living things, you know?"

"Words are living things?" My brain, a gray matter puddle of goo. "Words?" I said, my face scrunched into a question mark, an uninvited guest, yet one that adorned my countenance with dour regularity.

"Yes, *words*." The most powerful weapons in this world. You may have ignored how words have sentenced you to the lovely life you've lived since opening your big mouth at the *Welcoming Chaos* event, but they haven't ignored you. You, the ultimate fool, my egotistical friend," he said, his smirk a lethal weapon, "brandishing words as a tool of the apocalypse—"

"The apocalypse? How could—"

"Man, quit fucking about. Open your head. Dive inside and skinny dip in the facts. Aren't you paying attention?" Kerouac, or whatever he really was— an illusion or perhaps a nightmare cast in familiarity, all seemed quite possible— started to pace about, not like a lion anxious to get out of the cage, but one awaiting the trainer to shove a slab of meat in the cage... and to latch on to the arm of the trainer to sink his fangs into the point he was trying to get across to me. "Some words, some sequences of words, are dangerous. Apocalyptic. You welcomed the dark legions that gorged on the possibility of annihilation. You see, we enjoy the suffering of mankind at its own hands, means, and stupidity, but not enough to allow the end games to be played out." He shook his head enthusiastically, shaking a finger as well— no, *no!* "But some rogue members of our breed don't care. Burroughs stated that 'language is a virus from outer space.' He didn't realize how close he was to the truth. Some words *are* viral in inconceivable ways. Cataclysmic and suicidal fantasies are their method of spreading their nihilistic tendencies. The apocalypse would bring them euphoria beyond compare. We, the guardians, cannot allow this. We are a glutton for suffering and need the wings of torment and travesty to flutter eternally. Mind you, it's not easy keeping man's death wish quest at bay." He paused, absorbed by his thoughts, or the thoughts of the hive mind *we* he spoke of. "Our patience grows thin as the skin of a grape at the idiocy of such a self-destructive race, but our passion for its suffering supersedes our annoyance."

His words heavy as a dead body I carried because I had to, my cross made of flesh, the words I'd employed, nefarious. I knew what I was doing. I knew on that New Year's Eve what I was doing. I was opening doors. I was inviting the dark legions to take the reins and ride us into the sunset. My hatred for my fellow humans had peaked. I wanted them all gone.

I was Henry Coronado. I *am* Henry Coronado.

Impossible!

"Your rebellious quest was deterred before completion; otherwise we wouldn't even be having this conversation. As with the many before you who catered to similar anarchic ideals, you were relegated to an existence outside of the reality you knew."

"Outside of the reality I knew? Preposterous." I shoved my resignation aside, a phoenix rising up to lay claim to my sanity. "I live every day by my own means. I—"

"You call what you've been doing for over fifty years living? You're not that stupid, Henry. We aligned your monotonous existence on a plain outside of the world you had so wanted to destroy. You are caught in an endless loop of amnesia, faint recollection, obsession, research, and ultimately, rumor made real, yet fading with every passing second."

"My life as rumor. What lies you brandish. What ridiculous improbabilities. I spit in the face of this nightmare, anxiously waiting to wake from it in my bed—"

"In the cold, hard world of your deteriorating mind, your deteriorating memory; the world's deteriorating memory." As if on cue, under infinite black heavens— *I heard the scrambling of large animals above, many in force, a cacophonous din of unrelenting primitive guile: a massacre.*

Yet, I fervently denied everything!

"I will awaken and you will be nothing more than a pawn in Morpheus's devious machinations. Nothing more than dream dust scattered to the cranial dungeons."

"So poetic, your denial," he said, they said, the guardians. Making their point clear, Kerouac's face morphed and melted as wax beneath a lit wick, his body inflated, grew bulky in uneven increments— a distortion of process. Even the clothing shifted from his dark suit to a dark brown leather jacket, the material cracking as it stretched, the dead animal awakened only to cry out in agony. When the melting face recomposed itself before me into an even more familiar visage, I gasped.

"Randlebot!"

"No, just a tool in order to help your understanding. '*I am large, I contain multitudes.*' But heed my warning, as you refused to do when Randlebot was sent to correct your path. You are slowly fading into non-existence with every passing second. Soon, anyone who thought they remembered Henry Coronado and his poetry, specifically the ominous *invocation* that was *Autumn in the Abyss*, will have died. Ink in books will rearrange to recall nothing. Fade as you do, to nothing. You will have never existed. You will have never been thought. You—"

"Stop. This nightmare must stop! I must awaken and forget it all."

Randlebot... the Randlebot thing, laughed, bubbles over the edge of the pot, dark red and bleeding as a punctured artery.

"One last note. Your obsession is the Catch-22 of your personal hell. You see, my friend" —the words are laced with a trace of compassion, another lie, I was sure— "as long as you continue to believe in Henry Coronado, you keep the reality intact, no matter how parchment thin it is." He rubbed his thumb and two fingers together. "The only way it will ever stop is when you let go and let it drift away, man. Learn to forget. After years poisoning the space outside of the reality you knew, you will eventually fade, never to wake from the limbo of staring at blank walls for days, months, years— forever, man. Forever." He leaned forward and thrust his fist into his palm. That is the only way this will ever end. That is the only way you, Henry Coronado, will ever be set free." He snorted, a cat teasing a cornered mouse. Confirmation of the lie his bogus compassion expressed. "Some of us don't care whether you ever reach this realization. As mentioned, we thrive on mankind's suffering. You being a man in between, a man stuck, oh"—he quivered, a ripple of bliss, a caress of pleasure unimaginable— "your suffering brings such pleasure to us."

I clenched my eyelids as fists, a boxer ready to fight, damn it, fight. I had to wake up, had to extinguish this horrid nightmare from my system, my mind. I had to let it all go and start afresh with research that might lead to something that made sense. I had to—

—open my eyes and scream.

In the bathroom, the mirror I had broken years ago was solid, a lake of lies made icy at the center. I saw my reflection, fifty plus years on, Henry Coronado, once a handsome man, now resembling more a pile of excrement left to petrify on the lawn. My shape was huge and unruly. The hair atop my head jutted thick as rat's tails around my face twisting every which way, a barbed wire halo. The slope of my large shoulders suggested sloughed off glaciers settling into dead oceans, the glaciers made of flesh. Massive white rolls tattooed with blue veins and moles as thick as my pinky and a conglomeration of scars that resemble embroidered hieroglyphs radiated as languages long dead, a living death, the proof of the guardian's words. Dead yet alive; no, dead, yet existing, no real life here. My enormous belly spilled forth, blanched to transparent, the veins and organs and rattlesnake intestines roiling frantically, bruise-blue trimmed in decay-black faded into other hues within the rancid, rainbow spectrum causing my gorge to rise. I projectile vomited on the mirror, blotting out the image. Thankfully blotting out the image.

Yet within the stinking, dripping black discharge, faces took shape— Kerouac again, Burroughs and Breton, Catherton and Borges, Lovecraft and Ginsberg, Plath and Sexton and Rimbaud and DeVries and faces I did not recognize, their allegiance privy only to those who truly understood: the guardians and perhaps the dark legions. Perhaps many of these had ended up as me, pushing too far, too far...

And there was Randlebot again; a man I loved; a man I hated, my savior— the final nail in my splintered coffin— laughing.

But he was not alone now. They were all laughing at me, my eardrums swelling with their gruesome guffaws, all as if in on a secret I was only now beginning to understand.

The mayhem on the roof, a riotous racket, joined in the cackling sonic fray, deafening, determined.

I denied it all, leaning forward, lapping up their laughing faces, slurping and swallowing the lies with every slick caress of my tongue against the mirror... And the mirror itself; the glass cracked and crumbled in my eager mouth. My tongue and lips, a blind plastic surgeon's masterpiece. Blood smeared as comets flashing bright red across the mirror that remained only to be ingested with the next stroke of my crudely enthusiastic tongue. I devoured memory and lies and suggestions and fictions and silenced every laugh in the belly of the beast, this beast: Henry Coronado.

I howled, "Amen," as I finished my banquet. I smiled in the darkness, stumbled out of the room and waddled drunk on insanity as I made way to the bed. I tottered as the leaning tower of Pisa before my legs gave out and I landed on the floor, a fistful of blanket snagged to no avail. The crash shook me to the jiggling core. My abandoned soul scowled in a corner of the dark, below the now humming battle above, a static hum of the melee in motion put on hold, waiting, waiting...

~

My vision blurred, then sharpened, focused. I rose from the floor, not sure how I got there. Clumsy me. I strained as I do and tossed the blanket to the bed. It landed as a crescent, the shape of a toothless smirk. My lips and tongue ached as if shredded, but I ignored this and hobbled through the hallway toward the den, toward my computer. A package of uncooked ramen noodles awaited me. I tore into it, stuffed a fistful of noodles in my anxious maw. I tapped the mouse, shuffled it a bit more, and the monitor lit up. Alive.

Ready for my research.

Jogging my memory, moving the obsession to the front, the impression was vague at best, obscured by the muddle of dreamsickness that filled my thoughts with indistinct images

I sat there, crunching on dry ramen noodles, trying to remember who I was researching. Who and why. A name rose above the debris: Henry.

Henry who?

Circling and prying deep within, it finally came to me: Henry Coronado.

This information did not bring me comfort.

I entered "Henry Coronado poet" into the Google search engine.

There were no results.

I entered variations of this, to no avail.

I simpered meekly while the incessant tick tock traipse of the many clocks ricocheted off the walls around me— circling and prying deep within— signifying nothing more than my unfortunate existence.

I heard contented purring from above— the roof— and carried on.

Because my obsession grew crystalline, my obsession grew *teeth*. My obsession insisted without question. Only one thing mattered to me in this life...

I needed to know what happened to Henry Coronado.

> "I myself am an absolute abyss."
> —Antonin Artaud

Broken Teacup

"The path to knowledge is paved with the carcasses of experience."

With the statement, he could tell that it understood; shadows rippled as a smile from the void. It spoke:

"You will get me what I need, yes?"

"I will get you what you need."

~

"She's just lumpy, misshapen. You can't really want to—"

"She'll do, yeah. She'll do."

Lemmy and me, we'd been doing this gig for a few years, exploring the depths of perversion and presenting it in one form or another to those willing to pay the price for said perversity. We brought joy to the sickos of the world.

Why? Good question. It was primarily dark curiosity on my part. And the money, now that it'd started to kick in big time.

But for Lemmy it was different. He was just a walking hard-on at all hours.

I once told him, "You've got no soul," shaking my head at his impudence.

He responded with the expected crude rejoinder: "Who needs a soul when I've got a hole?" and proceeded to unload into any willing, unwilling, or just empty hole he could find.

A few years back, just out of high school, I'd been

headed for college— I got smarts but what I really wanted was experience— I was sidetracked by a bunch of noise bands that specialized in a kind of aural rape, bands like Whitehouse and their offshoot Sutcliffe Jugend, Smell & Quim, and the True Crime Electronics of Slogun. Lemmy and I decided to join the fray and make our own noisy excursions into the like-minded, sexually depraved world of our heroes.

Our kink was that we went for a kind of "real world" take on things, not exactly original but you had to start somewhere. We scraped the bowels of the small towns in Texas that we frequented for the lowest of the low hookers and suggested the most disgusting encounters imaginable. We taped the responses and even the encounters for use on our recordings. These tapes were manipulated and we added the appropriate noise accompaniment, guitar and bass cranked full throttle, creating a dense wall of sadistic sonics. The repetitious mayhem sounded like an orgy of hump happy monster trucks. We played up our roots calling ourselves Texas Chainsaw Erection. Our live reputation, replete with the most obscene video accompaniment, got us our first release, the underground classic, *Elbow Deep in Love*.

Heads turned but our pocketbooks still seemed in cahoots with the poverty line, and we needed money to pursue our interests.

One of the advantages of doing this kind of thing, specializing in such decadent ventures, was that it draws a unique fan base and from that fan base come unique requests.

People wanted to hear the most screwed up shit, but beyond that, we realized with the release of a couple of homemade video clips that what they really wanted was to see these things in full on, Technicolor clarity.

A thought about moving on to more lucrative endeavors

simmered between Lemmy and me, but we let it simmer, unformed, while we whipped out a couple more releases. They were the same old shit still limited in their scope.

Of course, we enjoyed making them. Our most famous track, "Curly Straw," included a Texas sweetie, twang and all. She was a skinny girl who did things you would not believe— flexible, she was. She claimed, "Hell, I'd suck the shit outta your asshole with a curly straw and a smile for that kinda money." We looped this and interjected bleats of the most dense, abusive noise you could imagine. The gist for us was our gleeful participation— we were nothing if not thorough— but something dark simmered under our glee. What simmered finally came to a head and demanded expression.

I remembered when it happened, one of those classic moments when one discards the parachute and takes a leap anyway.

Ain't life grand?

We'd noticed Black Hat at a few of our live shows. He had a look in his eyes that made me think he was in league with Lemmy. Like Lemmy he didn't have a soul, but he lacked Lemmy's sense of humor— the only thing that tethered Lemmy to some kind of humanity, lean as that was. I felt it swell, the cock in need of a stroke, and Lemmy pulled hard, without flinching.

Lemmy, cigarette dangling, to the point: "Whatcha *really* looking for, cowboy?"

Black Hat teetered. The unexpected question jostled his honed-to-a-laser-pin-point-focus on the screen behind us. The video playing between sets was culled from a Japanese old school classic, *Guinea Geisha*. I wasn't sure what episode, but the woman's just had her hands cut off and they did that questionable curl, closing like a dead spider, as if real.

Readjusting his focus to us, he steadied himself and

laid it out hardcore, no foreplay.

"I want a bitch to die at the end, after she does a horse."

It was boring, predictable. I somehow had expected more. We catered to our audience's requests, so bestiality was part of the action we were into. Our second release, *Squeal like a Pig*, was full of bestiality samples, which were a lot easier to get than you would think. The desperate would stoop to anything for whatever *they* needed.

The death thing was a place we had yet to explore.

Made me a little uncomfortable, so I popped a couple Rolaids, kept my mouth shut and listened to where this was going.

Lemmy dropped ash, not missing a beat: "How much you willin' to pay if we record this and put it on a DVD for you?"

Black Hat's eyes flickered with a light of euphoria so unmistakable that it was something I will never forget, like he came alive for the first time then and there. "Anything," he said.

The band died that day, and the new agenda took form: internet clips and D.I.Y. DVDs, driven now by *real* money. We recruited Elvis, a California computer whiz into our stuff— he had created a fan website for us, so we hired him to make it the authorized website— and started on the next stage of our sleazy careers.

The killing was odd in the beginning. No problem for Lemmy, but I only did a couple of girls before I realized that wasn't my thing. That said, most of these girls, hell, they haven't been living for a while, so it's not like they was missing anything important. It was not like their missing would be noticed.

The sordid requests that went with the killing, they were another story. Nothing too mind-bending— hell, they were going to die after all was said and done anyway. Nothing much we did beforehand could match that for visceral impact— but still... The usual included cut-and-dried fetishism, bestiality, coprophagy for the shit eatin' enthusiasts, piss drinking as well, BDSM, some double penetration stuff that turned into double anal, all the average extremes. All of it starred Lemmy and me and a couple of good old boys, Lance and Pete (whoever wasn't involved held the camera). We paid them off in free pussy and whatever they were drinking or chewing at the time. Kept the real profits for ourselves.

We had Elvis do his magic; keep us so under the radar you'd need sonar to know anything about us. It was a dicey sleight of hand, took a series of passwords to get in, switching daily. Visitors needed encrypted codes, decrypted codes, synchronized watches and more. They had to jump through flaming hoops, give up their first born, if it was a female we could eventually defile— just to get in. I was amazed that anybody ever got in. I couldn't picture anybody being able to enter all of this with one saliva slick hand on their joint while they typed with the other, but they did; these boys were hungry.

Those who really cared found their way.

On the two year anniversary of the site, we headed to the East Bay of northern California to officially meet Elvis, the third part of our triumvirate, and to check out the nightlife, so to speak.

It was a road trip in search of fresh meat. Now, here's the gist: in Texas, the core hooker populace was skinny girls, really young, bad teeth. They were freewheeling girls who don't give a fuck. They do whatever it takes to get the meth they needed. Hell, they were willing and able and even if not so able, they would anyway.

Louisiana has some dark-skinned pieces of meat that really put up a fight once the hammer came down. That made for one of our most popular downloads, "Hammerhead Splatterfuck," the one where we offed the big legged bitch mid-orgasm and, realizing she's about to be offed, she fought like a champ.

Lemmy still proudly flaunted the scars he got from that one.

But the East Bay, this place has some real disgusting, let it all go and still think they were hot shit hookers. Cruising down East 14th in Oakland and San Leandro, changing from that to Mission Boulevard in Hayward, and back up to Oakland, we got the real class of the class, cream of the crop, the top load winner. This bitch that Lemmy was checking out had no shape, no discernable age— no nothing to indicate that she was human. She was disgusting on a level that made even me want to puke. And he's thinking his always erect dick will find pleasure in her hole. It must be some kind of wayward repugnance that got him hot and bothered, that made it okay to fuck her as long as he got to off her afterward. Straightforward cum 'n' kill exercise, nothing special, more to keep the edge on and maybe give Elvis a bit of a thrill by letting him witness an actual performance.

But then it came to me, as I scrolled through the notes on my cell, we had a request for humiliation, mutilation, torture and death from a mysterious Mr. Liu— as if this formal declaration of self meant anything to us. We called him Mr. Liu to his face over the web cams, but in spite of his pretentious manner his nattily attired ass was deep down just like the rest of them fucks who got their rocks off on this kind of sick stuff. He was a reclusive self-made millionaire, but that was all the info we could get out of him or that Elvis could find. We were wary at first because we usually needed a whole lot more info before letting somebody into the fold or onto the website, but his perseverance made it apparent he was just some horny old Chinese guy looking for that "special something" that would rouse his aged pecker to life.

Whatever. As soon as we found out specs and that he was willing to pay big bucks, we moved him to the front of the line. No waiting. Let's take care of this boy ASAP.

He was going to pay two-hundred fifty thousand dollars, our biggest take yet. Seems like we could have set our own prices? Hell no, we lost more than we got, but this one had teeth. With the aforementioned specs and his insistence that the act had to be performed in a room with only one light, making it hard to film because of all shadows and such, it seemed authentic. Maybe the grittiness was part of his kink, or maybe he was trying to deny what he actually was paying for: murder. Long drawn out murder. This one had resonance and we could tell it wasn't bullshit.

Passé, yes, what with those torture porn movies like *Saw* and *Hostel* leading the way, or some of that old school Japanese seriously screwed up shit like *Guinea Geisha* and *Delicate Flower*, but if that's what two-hundred fifty thousand wants, that's what two-hundred fifty thousand gets.

"If you're gonna do her, we should do it as per the request from Mr. Liu. You know what I'm talking about."

Lemmy scratched his crotch, more like fondled himself, and said, "Not this one. I want somebody feelin' the streets in her smile for that one. I think Mr. Liu would really like it that way..." He clenched his fist, as if one dead bitch or another really mattered, but I dug his determination. "Maybe he'd get off on more of the same. If he's got the money and inclination to throw it our way, well... I mean, this fat bitch, she's got nothing for him to get off on, she's humiliating just to look at. We could off her for sport, y'know? And make a few bucks, kind of a promo deal on the site, right, Elvis?"

Elvis' eyes' glazed. "Yeah, do her. Let me watch you do her... live."

Elvis was zoned.

Lemmy looked primed as though he knew the evening's

entertainment was already aligned.

Mr. Liu would have to wait.

Later that week, after we gave Elvis a show he would not soon forget (along with a souvenir clit ring still dappled in blood), as we were cruising again along that same desolate stretch of road— Sunday morning, probably too early for the churchgoers, but not so early as to surprise— I spotted the perfect victim.

"There. Over there. Look at her."

"What? It's Sunday morning and there ain't no hookers—"

"Fuck that, she's lookin' for some action. She's perfect, look at her."

I was smitten by this dyed blond bitch with a rockin' shape looking all nervous and shit. If she's hooking, it's clear she's not been at it for long, that's for sure. She's got victim stamped onto her corneas with that pleading look.

"She's perfect. Look at her eyes. Check out that desperate look. She really needs something, boys. And that smile, kind of like a broken teacup, some kind of beautiful design scarred, chipped. She's barely hanging on. Can't you see it? Can't you see her future, peering into the broken teacup and reading the tea leaves and there's nothing left but this dismal existence...?"

Lemmy pulled the car past her into the Lucky grocery store parking lot. I know I looked hard at her when we passed by, so obvious what she was doing. The brakes squealed as we stopped and the car felt hot, like death and sex and more death just waiting to be distributed.

"Well, Shakespeare, I think your eloquent description is a prime example of what Mr. Liu is looking for, so I'll—"

"No, I'll get her. I'll... do her. I'll give Mr. Liu everything he wants, and more."

"What the fuck, you gonna get your hands dirty, eh?"

Without looking at him, and with no malice: "Fuck you.

I've killed before. Just because you get most of that out of the way don't mean I won't do it again. Like now."

"Don't scrunch your scrotum, pal. She's yours."

I was love-struck, but my love was dangerous. Everything about this damaged bitch had my balls tingling and my cock starting to strain in my jeans.

I leaned out the passenger side window, waved her over. She was still looking at me; I saw an impression of a smile caress her lips, not really taking hold. God damn, this was too easy— and I wanted her. Something in me really wanted to destroy her, break her into a thousand little pieces.

Sure, I wanted to fuck her as well, but that look, those eyes, that "special something" that Mr. Liu would really enjoy lurked in those eyes.

She walked briskly toward the car. That smile etched on her face took hold, but it was different now. Her broken teacup countenance was still present, but there was some-thing *amiss* in that smile.

As she got close to the car, her stride grew strong. Something in me grew uneasy, angry, confused. I still wanted her, but something rang hard in my ears.

"You are the one who will teach me of love," she said, left hand soft against my cheek. I turned away, toward Lemmy, who had a Cheshire Cat grin on his face. She put her right hand on my other cheek and pulled me to her again, so I could see her up close, take in her flawed beauty.

"You are the one who will love me forever, yes?" Not really a question, more a statement, but I answered her in the appropriate manner.

"Yeah, I love you long time, baby."

Lemmy laughed, Elvis too.

I grinned, a wolf in sheep's clothing.

She seemed satisfied with the response.

"Switch," I said, signaling Elvis to ride shotgun while I

romanced Broken Teacup in the backseat. I took her hand and pulled her into our love nest.

"You want to know about love? I'll show you all about love."

I kissed her hard, her mouth seeming surprised as if she'd never been kissed before. I normally wouldn't kiss them, but this one— it seemed like the right thing to do. And I wanted to.

I was all out of kilter.

We drove toward a house Elvis had borrowed for the occasion from another fan, a guy on vacation; fifteen minutes max and we were there. The whole time I had kissed her and she had seemed to grow more comfortable with the idea as she caught on, kissing me back. She tasted like she'd eaten dust for days, but she tongue wrestled with enthusiasm so I didn't mind much.

"This place smells rank, dude," Lemmy said, stating the obvious.

The smell was moldy. I couldn't imagine anybody living there.

"Didn't smell this bad earlier when I fixed up the basement with the stuff you wanted," Elvis said, nostrils flaring and face crinkling in disgust.

Broken Teacup didn't seem to notice or care. What she did do was keep pulling my face to hers, so insistent.

Desperation had nothing on her.

"You will show me more of love, yes?"

"You talk funny, no?" Lemmy teased her as we headed for a door leading to the basement.

She tilted her head in a queer way and looked at him with a trace of something I'd call hate, yet it was like it was unborn, this hate, as if she didn't know how to convey it.

I sure was picking up a lot of weird vibes from her.

"This way," Elvis said, leading us toward the back of the house. The furniture looked ratty and worn, yet it still seemed like nobody had been there for quite some time.

"How long has your buddy been on vacation?"

Elvis ignored Lemmy's query and unlocked a door. Wooden planks creaked as we stepped downstairs into darkness.

"And God said, 'Let there be light,' and there was light." After waving his hand around, Elvis found a string and pulled it. One dim bulb semi-lit the room.

"You will love me here?" Broken Teacup asked.

"Apparently I will." The room was done up right. One bed, leather straps to bind her and the glimmering suggestion of metallic implements in the shadows along the wall, promising many hours of fun.

She grabbed my arm and pulled me to her, forcefully kissing me. "I like this," she said, and I knew she was a goner for good. If she didn't pick up on what was happening here, it would only make taking her that much more satisfying. She may be hot, but her idiosyncrasies and general naïveté would make me nauseated if she hung around for too long.

One day here should do the trick.

The camera sat on a tripod in the corner next to the barely perceptible shiny stuff meant for cutting and tearing; severing. Elvis fidgeted with it, and I heard the low hum of its operation.

We'd planned this all out. I knew my part now that I was the ringleader; Lemmy and Elvis awaited my command.

The bed and straps were empty but soon they would be filled.

"You ready, boys?" I rubbed my hands together then unsnapped my jeans.

"It's time I showed you all about love, Broken Teacup."

Lemmy snorted. "Broken Teacup, Christ, Bobby, that's rich."

Elvis grabbed her left arm.

She turned to him and said, "No." The word slid kind of funny out of her lips, and all of a sudden, Elvis shriveled up, shrinking on the spot into a hairless rodent-like thing, except the eyes were huge, and hanging by tendrils. He... it... *he* scrabbled in circles at her feet, unable to break the cycle because both eyes hung slack to one side, weighing him down.

"Fuck!" Lemmy kneeled down and pulled the knife from his boot, raising up with it underhanded, going for her stomach.

Broken Teacup put her palm up like a cop directing traffic.

Lemmy froze before some invisible force flung him to the mattress. The straps came alive and wrapped tight around his arms and legs. He let out a yell, almost my name, but then the sound corkscrewed into his torso, and his arms seemed to crackle and fizz, morphing into a bunch of large cockroaches. The legs followed suit. His head sagged like a punctured balloon, but his face took the down escalator into the pit of his torso where a bunch of cocks and assholes materialized all over the mass of mutating flesh. His clothing had turned brittle and flaked away. This thing, Lemmy, Christ, the cockroaches all had cocks like barbed razors and took to humping every orifice on his body. And there were plenty of them. Holding themselves steady, the cockroaches grasped his many cocks as they pummeled his many bleeding assholes. He was ejaculating in both pleasure and agony and the whole thing made me turn away and throw up.

I felt like I was spewing lava, yet I didn't want it to stop. I wanted to burn away the obscenities I had just witnessed, and which still screamed, filling my ears with the shock of confusion, agony, and physical degeneration. My mind couldn't conceive of changes of this magnitude. Was Lemmy still able to breathe and sense it all?

"His soul is very disgusting," Broken Teacup said.

"What the fuck are you talking about? *What the fuck are you?*" I cowered below her, knees grinding the concrete floor as I shimmied away.

"You will show me love now... yes?"

I looked in her eyes and that scarred innocence shone through.

Then something more shook the foundation of my sanity. The shadows to my right roiled and groaned.

Broken Teacup looked toward the screaming thing that was Lemmy and said, "Shhhhh." She turned back to me, not to the shadows.

The sudden hush ached in my ears. A moment later the vacuum seeped away and I could hear my harsh, quickened breath.

I watched as the shadows dilated and a man leaned out of them without actually leaving their embrace, nattily attired as always.

"Mr. Liu?"

"As you can tell, Mr. Rickart..."

He leaned back and I could no longer see him. Silence muted every sound, as if my head were dipped in mud. I had a moment to somehow think of my usual response to being called, Mr. Rickart: *Mr. Rickart's my daddy, motherfucker. My name's Bobby, don't you forget it*. But he realized this was not the place for idiotic responses.

No way.

He leaned forward again; I heard static dancing in his voice, like guitar feedback tuned down low as he continued.

"...you are in a most precarious situation."

He hung there, as if he had adjusted to the space he occupied; it was now his space, here in this bleak basement hell.

"I am here to clean up the mess, Mr. Rickart. We humans are so messy and that is not acceptable. There are others who do not appreciate it. But there are also others who find deep fascination with us humans."

Something started to hiss on both sides of Mr. Liu.

"Just a moment, please," he said, his head nodding left and right, acknowledging that which hissed in the darkness beside him.

The hissing grew in volume. It sounded obstinate, insistent.

Mr. Liu's head dipped ever so slightly. I got the impression that, despite appearances, he was not the one running the show.

"Very well," he said, leaning back into the shadows.

A brutal cacophony erupted. It brought incinerator heat with it as it surrounded me. Layer upon amplified layer struggled for dominance. Some sounds I knew: the dull crack of a pipe breaking bone; the gagging protest of the cock-filled throat; the meaty rhythmic drone of genitalia in full on fuck mode. Other sounds made sense within this din, and somehow I knew them as well: the joyous diseased blossom that blooms in the heart of those whose hunger can only be sated with suffering; the slow gnawing mastication of mental decay; the abysmal ache of emptiness that was the lonely heart.

The need for love, to know it and to understand it.

The sounds had purpose, as if they were alive and felt, wanted— *needed*. But I also understood that these perceptions were peripheral, because they were only reflections of those who occupied this room. Those I knew— Lemmy, Elvis and me— as well as Broken Teacup, and that which abandoned the shadows—the giants—are part of the noise.

As these thoughts assaulted me with the sheer ferocity of their decibel straining impressions, two headless giants marched with determination out of the shadows, their girth devouring the room. Each of their bodies was chiseled muscle. Each arm was tattooed with intricate designs.

Dragon's heads snapped and spat fire as they came alive at the fists.

One of the giants approached Elvis. The dragon of its right fist snatched him up and tossed him into the excavated bone and viscera bound cage that was its belly. Its neck stump tilted back, opened as a volcano, and black goo pulsed out over its broad shoulders and down its sculpted mass.

The other giant did the same with Lemmy. The black goo poured out of the stump, as if it experienced immense pleasure from the attainment of Lemmy.

Lemmy mouthed a soundless protest, eyes wide, yet vacant: nobody's home. Insanity was the stranger who wandered in the dark halls now.

As the giants backed into the shadows, the din was quieted by a muffled snick, as if a lock had sealed the cages shut.

Silence again, except in my throbbing skull.

Broken Teacup hadn't taken her eyes off me since silencing Lemmy, despite the commotion.

A moment later, Mr. Liu leaned out of the shadows again. A trickle of sweat ran along his cheek.

"You have an opportunity, Mr. Rickart. As you can see by the previous few minutes' demonstration, this is an opportunity you are not wise to ignore."

"What the fuck is going on?" I was still on my knees, crying now, my fear a palpable presence in the room.

Mr. Liu sighed. "As bad a soul as you are and what *it* can do to you..."

He nodded toward Broken Teacup, the woman standing above me; the woman who was obviously not a woman.

"Complying with this request is your only opportunity to... redeem yourself, or, at least, avoid the fate bestowed on your cohorts."

He nodded to the shadows.

I knew that I was a bad person, or at least a messed up person who had chosen a path that led me here. I wanted nothing to do with revealing that which was my soul.

"Why me?" I sobbed, trying to quiet my tears, snuffing them out as best as possible.

"I chose you because no matter how bad or misdirected a person is, some people are salvageable. I'm not saying you are one of those, Mr. Rickart, but maybe it is possible that you can attain a kind of dignity amidst the chaos, within what is left of your existence. It wants to learn something you might not even have the slightest idea about," he said, eyes darting in the direction of Broken Teacup, "but since you are a human, and my role is to assist in its goals while keeping the universe in balance, I will grant you this one opportunity to get it right in your life.

"The path to wisdom is paved with the carcasses of experience... and you have so much more to experience, Mr. Rickart."

Broken Teacup surprisingly turned to Mr. Liu and asked, "I thought the path to *knowledge* was paved with the carcasses of experience, yes?" She seemed distracted by semantics: wisdom, knowledge— what difference did it make?

Mr. Liu confirmed my suspicions with his next statement and the slim smile curling at the corner of his lips that accompanied it.

"All paths are paved with the carcasses of experience."

The words sent a chill through my already wracked body and mind. This experience, one to change the path of my life.

"Do you understand what I am saying, Mr. Rickart?"

I couldn't speak, my mind reeling, my thoughts bumper car crashing in my head.

Broken Teacup turned to me then, both hands on my moist cheeks and said, "You will show me love now."

I understood this was my opportunity.

I saw black gulfs glisten like polished slate in her eyes.

Maybe there was something salvageable; maybe there was something for me to learn as well.

"Yes," I said, as my voice cracked. "Yes, I will show you love."

She smiled and her fleshy disguise started to melt.

It did not matter what it revealed. I had only one option. I would show it love.

I would have to learn how, if I didn't want to end up like the others.

La mia immortalità

"Why don't you speak to me?" Samuel yelled, as the hammer smashed into the marble with a dull thump. He let the hammer drop out of his moist fingers. He released the chisel from his straining grip as well. As the dead weight of the hammer clunked onto the concrete floor, the tinny intonations of the chisel echoed weakly, a call and response wrought in frustration.

He wandered to a window, its panes sweating with condensation. The dreary, late summer chill outside unable to chip away at the heat inside the studio, or his veins.

"I thought you'd be well into the heart of this one by now, Sam." Claire's firm, polished glass timbres filtered into his ears, out of the blue— more so, the gray black overcast— not even knocking.

Samuel sighed, the weight of it all a burden Atlas would fail in lifting.

At forty-five years old, Samuel Nisi was a successful artist, first as a photographer, and then with oil paintings, old school by today's deluge of digital dregs, and embraced by a world stepping back to appreciate genuine artistry. Yet the fickle aspect of his desire for everlasting fame— in spite of his quality work with skills apparent yet not harnessed to maximum results— kept him searching for something more, something to really leave his imprint on the world.

He found his way to a studio near Rome, Italy— to be near the masters, his only true Gods, Michelangelo and

Bernini. The solitude was necessary for more reasons than would seem obvious. His aspirations had grown cunning. He would attain his goals at any cost, which had cost him friends, colleagues, personal relationships— not that they mattered to him. Anything that got in the way of his life's purpose, as whittled to spear sharp intensity as the years tolled, was easily discarded.

Seven years ago he'd taken up sculpting. The sculptures he created combined the power and majesty of mythical gods, goddesses and monsters with dirt-under-the-fingernails modern sensibilities. He had a love of those who lived by tooth, nail, and brass knuckles. The wealth of critical applause he garnered validated his personal artistic progression, but for Samuel, it was not enough. All art came easy to him, yet no art satisfied his lust for immortality. Sure, some of the sculptures may last forever, but none struck him as extraordinary. He still felt emotionally distanced from them, as if something, some scrap of magic, was missing— which irked him to no end.

Hence, he found his latest commission especially intriguing.

He was desperately in need of inspiration that took him beyond the norm, beyond anything he'd ever conceived. As if answering his wishes, the letter had come to him via the post, not even electronically, as most communication was conducted nowadays.

A new client by the name of Mr. Liu had requested a decidedly atypical commission, one whose ambiguity intrigued Samuel. It was simple, direct, the essence relayed in measured lines, as if Mr. Liu was a man of few words, yet knew exactly what he wanted... yet what he wanted, because of the vagueness of the details, inspired. Mr. Liu would send Samuel a large block of marble, "the rarest Carrara marble," he'd said, and it would be up to Samuel to "find whatever strange, lost soul was buried within the marble. Find what lives and breathes there and to bring it to the surface." That was all, no specifics, yet the money Mr. Liu was willing to spend, as well as how it touched a nerve within Samuel— more so, because of the latter— moved this to the top of his "to-do" list.

He had his latest girlfriend, Claire, one in a long line of art lovers who, once spending any amount of time with him, would realize that art was his lover and she was there as a vessel of his occasional physical passion or verbal abuse, research Mr. Liu, with minimal results. The phrase, "wealthy Chinese gentleman," seemed prevalent in search results, yet no source for his wealth was to be gleaned. Only one badly lit black and white photo, his features indistinct, though a trace of something Samuel thought of as world weariness and deep knowledge reflected in his eyes. He was an enigma, making an enigmatic proposition: to find the enigma within the marble.

Fine by Samuel: *open to interpretation.* Yet the act of putting the hammer to the chisel and the chisel to the marble inspired nothing but frustration. His muse was on vacation, something he'd never experienced before. Which surprised him even more, since the huge block of marble that had been delivered a week ago filled him with anticipation.

Most of the time, he worked with marble that featured, ever so slightly, the promise of smooth finality. This one had only the promise on display. Besides a perfectly flat foundation, the whole of what amazed him was the smooth, curved body, as if another sculptor had sheared off the edges, delineating an oval shape, and stopped, backed away, probably because he could not find the soul of this wondrous rock, either. When Samuel stroked it, placed his cheek to it in getting to know it— a ritual he'd undertaken with all blocks of marble— the sensations he felt were all wrong. Colder. Alien, he thought.

Yet when he circled it, looking for an opening, a way in— *for inspiration*— every step forward led to two steps back, and more contemplation. Where to begin? Though he'd worked marble hundreds of times without issue, something of the difference here gave him reason to pause.

But these sensations only urged him onward: he would not give in. He would listen with his hands, his anxious soul; he would listen or force it to talk to him, damn it!

"Honey," Claire said, drawing him away from his fragmented thoughts.

Not wanting to deal with any distractions and, really, that's mostly what she was at this point, Samuel said, "Can't get anything done with all these interruptions." He hadn't turned to face her, yet registered her heavy sigh.

"Fine. I can see you're in your usual cheerful mood, but I have something of importance to discuss with you."

"Something of importance?"

Another upscale art opening? Favors for whom, this time? He turned to see her, this beautiful, slender woman upon which, despite the chill outside, a lavender summer dress sprinkled with brilliant yellow Van Gogh sunflowers hung with luxurious perfection. She'd braided a matching bandana through her auburn hair. Lovely, but since they'd been together, her cheeks had grown cliff-sheared edges. Wasn't his fault, was it? Couldn't be. Even if he was a sculptor.

He smiled at the thought.

"Funny? What's funny, dear?" She moved closer to him, arms reaching awkwardly toward him, an insect quality laced into the movements as if she were hungry for something he no longer had the capacity to give to her: compassion, or even warmth.

Samuel ignored her, as he had work to do, a legacy to create. "What's so important that it can't wait until later?"

"It's been later the last three times I've attempted this

conversation, Sam. We need to talk now, before it gets... too late." Her eyes narrowed, silently pleading.

"Too late? The only thing that may ever be too late, my dear, Claire, is my appointment with destiny, distracted to derailment by the likes of, well"— sneering as he said it, an asp about to strike— "people like you. People in general. People— what a pitiable race to be associated with."

The moment hung heavy, the humidity eating comfort with the ravenous appetite of a flame to the wooden match beneath it.

With tears welling in her eyes, the light reflecting off the glossy azure orbs as sunlight on Caribbean seas, Claire blurted as if she could hold it in no longer, "I'm pregnant, Sam. I'm pregnant with our child, one of those people you so despise."

"For fuck's sake, just get an abortion—"

"An abortion?" Samuel watched her face crumble, like so many of the ruins that littered the Roman countryside. "You egotistical bastard. Your seed grows in my womb and you want me to cut it out and throw it away with the morning trash. How can you be so cruel?" She rubbed her belly. Samuel thought the affectation artificial. He shook his head in disgust.

He turned away, eyes on the window, taking in the rain as it kicked into high gear. In the distance, thunder rumbled, a vicious yet appropriate punctuation to his dismay.

"It's your child, Sam. We are going to be parents."

"Claire, I don't care what's inside you. I only care about what's inside that." He jerked his thumb toward the block of marble. "The last thing I want is to bring somebody else into this godforsaken world."

"Godforsaken or not, you shit, I'm pregnant and you must deal with this—"

"I'm not the one who's pregnant, Claire. That's *your* problem. *You* deal with it. I have my destiny to define."

She barked a laugh of derision.

"Your destiny. Your damned destiny has driven you to be a hateful human being. You're all ego, no heart."

Samuel paced as she spoke with such vitriol— she did not understand him. Would anybody? Was his goal of immortality one destined to fail, sinking into the swamp of worthless shit this meager race wallowed in?

No matter, he let the asp strike.

"It is the only consequence in this fallacy of an existence"—taking aim at her, sinking the fangs in with fervor— "but this fallacy of a relationship has run its course and if you want to have a bastard as evidence of our time together, by all means, squeeze that puppy out, but don't bring it around for me to see or to hear its whimpering cries or"—he picked up the hammer, his grip bleaching his knuckles white— "I'll find reason to put it to sleep forever."

Samuel let the demon within fuel his rage and welcomed its fury.

Claire backed away, slowly at first, trapped in the laser beam hatred of his stare.

As her foot met the chisel, her ankle twisted and she tumbled to the marble's base.

From his perch above her, lava filling his veins, he allowed the most malicious part of himself room to frolic.

"Perhaps I should make sure for good that there's no baby to interfere, eh, darling?" His lips peeled back as he bared his teeth. The demon was a rabid dog, a blood-crazed shark. He watched as Claire turned to crawl from him as his laughter dressed the room in the buzzing intonations of murder.

The thunder rumbled as ripped metal and gained foothold around them. It grew to a roar, something throaty and seething with its own black intent.

Lightning flashed white hot at the windows, then swallowed all light from the studio down its gleaming throat, lips clamped shut. The darkness was beyond birth and nightmare. This darkness promised complete soul annihilation.

Claire screamed and screamed again, as if her fear lodged as a needle stuck in the groove of a darkness swelling with insidious designs.

A voice cut like a machete into the soft belly of the ripe, juicy melon; not unpleasant, peculiar. The voice wavered as did the image— Samuel thought of celluloid strung through a dying camera. "Claire, it's time for you to go," the voice said. "You won't want to witness this. You and your son, Marshall..."

"Marshall. His name will be Marshall? I will have a boy?"

A small figure leaned over and offered his hand to help her to her feet.

"Marshall is my father's name. He was a good and kind man."

"I know," said the small figure. "I know."

"Mr. Liu?" Samuel said miffed to the teeth, uncertain of how he had gotten here. The shadows in the corner held no doorway.

Mr. Liu continued to flicker as he led Claire to the stairs. "Samuel will not be of any consequence in your child's life, but remember, he is your child. Not his. He will grow up to be a man of worth. Go now, and never look back."

"Thank you," she said, her words barely audible, eyes glazed as if drugged, as she drifted down the stairs.

Mr. Liu turned from her as she descended and went immediately toward Samuel. His gait was easy, confident. His stern features bore the weight of the task at hand, screwed tight into unsmiling stone.

Mr. Liu's flickering appearance downshifted into a lazy strobe, exposing sporadic glimpses of the marble's now malleable consistency. Malleable and seemingly alive.

"She won't remember a thing after your crude, heartless

exhibition, Mr. Nisi." Samuel peripherally noticed the agile fingers of Mr. Liu's right hand as they seemed to roll invisible coins between them as he spoke. "She will wake after many hours of sleep and remember telling you she was pregnant. She'll remember your negative response, but that is all. Tired of your dispassionate ways, she will move out of the apartment you share and move on for the sake of the boy." Mr. Liu shifted his gaze to the marble.

The dozens of questions that had initially filled Samuel's head, most of all, about Mr. Liu's mysterious appearance, fell by the wayside, sinking as an anchor, never to be dredged up. The amorphous wonder held him enraptured. This living marble held the key to his immortality. When he touched it, he felt as well as heard, the sonorous chants course through his marrow, fluttering at the ridge of his tympanic membranes.

Thunder roared again, the voluminous voice of the void opening wide to gulp down the morsel. The wooden beams above cracked and rippled as liquid, a stone kissing the surface of the serene lake.

"Those who require balance within the universe have a perverse sense of humor, Mr. Nisi. I am their liaison here on earth. The last link to logic you will not comprehend." He sighed, as though his motivation was dictated by others. "As if your understanding matters to them. It's merely my job to relay these messages. None of this will make sense to you, except perhaps the final result."

The beams began to splinter, cracking as the joints of weary giants.

The thunder growled, an impossible, strident reverberation reeled in from the limitless expanse of the cosmos' deepest back alley chasms, jolting Samuel from his trance-like obsession.

Turning to Mr. Liu, he noticed how the pulsing strobe, fluid and prismatic, had moved from his flesh and now resided in his eyes. Bright colors and damaged hues streamed out with the wriggling motivation of eels.

Mr. Liu was right: if there was logic here, it could not be a logic that even matters to him, what with the strange, hallucinatory folly he was presently experiencing. The rules he understood held no sway here. As he went to pull away from the marble, to abandon this madness and make a hasty exit, he was stymied. His fingers remained glued to the marble.

Mr. Liu backed away, dropping the invisible coins. Samuel thought he heard the metallic clink as they kissed the floor. "Mr. Nisi, you've turned from human into monster over the years. This monster would inhibit the aspirations of a young boy whose destiny matters to this world."

"What the hell is going on with my..." Samuel twisted, pulling hard, but with every effort, his hand was sucked deeper into the quicksand of the marble. Worse yet, the process began to peel his flesh and pulverize the bones beneath.

He screamed. His scream expressed true agony, a pain worthy of admiration.

Samuel forced "Help me" from his throat, yet no help would be had. He watched as Mr. Liu slinked back to his hidden doorway in the intersection of here and there.

Mr. Liu continued: "But those who preside over such things have decided to grant you your wish, Mr. Nisi. They require balance." With that, he ducked into the shadows, as if seeking refuge, as though this were his hub of relative safety.

The more Samuel struggled, the swifter he was devoured by the marble. But the bottomless pit of pain required struggling. He had to give all of himself to this piece.

All of himself.

Despite his predicament, Samuel was momentarily

distracted as he watched the rafters rattle and burst sky-ward, enthusiastically gulped into the black heavens above. Stars winked into non-existence, magnifying the depth of infinite space. Wood wailed in splintered defeat, the sound slipping preposterously into metallic registers before mutating into cadences that hinted at the tearing of meat from the broken bones of fallen prey.

The insistence of the roar roughly shoved aside the clouds. The impossible scenario witnessed by eyes wide with panic and ears praying for silence suggested truths the mad display confirmed. Everything he thought he knew was false or at least altered.

From around the ragged edges of the displaced roof where cilia trembled violently as if being whipped by a cosmic wind of immense power, weird, aberrant geometric shapes waterfalled into the gaping wound of the vacated roof. Shining as shards of stars, they splatted in oily pools, reconstituting instantly, shifting between cube and octagon and triangle and so many more geometric shapes. Their cries reverberated between the slim film of the murmur and the blunt, pot-holed skin of the lie.

The form's stench clogged his nostrils with the vile afterbirth stew of their incessant breeding. Each impact constituted a rebirth of hideous objectives, the details of which his mind ached not to imagine.

They were precursors to a truth Samuel did not want to engage.

Swarming around the base of the marble and flowing into it, these monstrosities enhanced the process in progress, ratcheting the pain to excruciating levels.

Samuel's mind floundered for thoughts that made sense.

At the center of this sentient wasteland, something that could only be thought of as "it" throbbed and shimmered. It blinked and blinked again as it took him in.

From beyond perception, contemplation, and oblivion it approached: squirming, rotating feverishly, folding into itself as it flowered outward, a diseased, kaleidoscopic maelstrom regurgitating constantly. It spun faster as it advanced. The pinprick at the center of it all opening as a predatory aperture, an iris dilating at the insistence of such desolate, immeasurable space and fierce desire.

Samuel thought— God?— and laughed, delirious now. His laughter died. Yes, perhaps this was God. What other being could perform with such awe-inspiring panache? He gibbered piecemeal prayers until they crumbled at the feet of incomparable fear. God approached at blinding speed, the blurred countenance gaining burnished clarity. It had a purpose here, that Samuel would never know or understand or even have the time to consider— only experience. Struggling harder, his face peeled as the marble ingested him, yet as his final scream redefined terror and dread for those who enjoyed such discoveries, he could not pull his gaze from that which contaminated the whole of his vision. He stared as his eyes bled and he could not deny the horrific veracity of what he saw, *what he saw...*

Then silence...

...and infinite blackness: such dense, ebony beauty, such a grand obscene vista...

These were his thoughts during his last few seconds in the flesh before all sanity was wiped from his cranial blackboard.

~

Hours later, before dawn, Mr. Liu stood in front of Samuel Nisi's masterwork. He already knew its history, the astonished reception it would reap.

A modern masterpiece incorporating a

depth of emotion Nisi's previous art barely acknowledged.

On par with Edvard Munch's "The Scream," although the choice to make himself the subject and the three-dimensional aspect of marble sculpture gives it more resonance.

This shockingly realistic depiction of an unseen horror left to the imagination of the individual, as rendered by troubled artist, Samuel Nisi, is sure to transcend time...

On and on, it was the art world event of the year, the decade. It would persevere forever, a landmark work, *the* landmark work of the 21st century.

Mr. Liu canted his head toward the sculpture, sweat beading at his brow as he listened to the thin exhalation of Samuel Nisi's final scream from within the marble prison. A sound only he could hear, a forbidding present handed down from his employers.

A sound that would linger evermore.

"We are much alike, Mr. Nisi," he said, his voice a notch above a whisper. "We are men who squandered our humanity in order to gain immortality. But I received an opportunity of the rarest sort amidst times of internal chaos." His bleakest memories bloomed, corrosive, famished, but he refused to feed them now, or ever again. It was part of the price he paid for his immortality— this battle. "You would never have gotten back to yours."

He knelt down and ran his fingers over the base, as his employers had insisted. Letters took shape beneath his moist caress.

La mia immortalità. My Immortality.

He thought he heard thunder laughing in the distance,

but the storm had passed. His work was done. He left Samuel Nisi to his singular torment— the fulfilment of his life's goal— as he strode dispassionately toward an invisible door between here and there and awaited his next assignment.

Becoming Human

Detective Roberto "Bobby" Vera clenched his large, gnarled fists, then opened them wide and took the bottle of whiskey in one hand, the shot glass in the other. He set the glass down and tipped the bottle against his eager lips. He needed the burn. He needed to have his insides cauterized by the harsh liquid. He set the bottle down, head swimming in dismal thoughts, drowning in the knowledge of what came next. Moving the mouse, he clicked on the arrow to the video clip sent to him by a copycat killer, rapist, and worse— a strange statement, but Vera understood the vile contingencies of "worse;" it crippled his every thought— and cursed God, cursed his mere existence, and cursed the deranged déjà vu mockery playing out before him on the monitor.

He set out on his path to the abandoned factory in northern California immediately after watching the clip. He had done this before. Done *exactly* this before. It may have been a different factory the first time, but the gist of what was in motion was a perfect reproduction. What he'd just watched looked like the work of the fiend from that other time.

His primary thought was that, despite the spot-on similarities, he could not let it reach a similar finality. This time there would be no questions asked, no chance for this bleak acolyte to weave his heinous philosophy into Vera's now broken mind. He would unload the whole magazine into the madman and walk away. Though he'd been working with the FBI once the copycat crimes had commenced, and he was contacted by this unoriginal yet still quite lethal perpetrator for the finale, he needed no interference.

Now... now he had to be alone to deal with this as he knew he must. He saw no other way, having spent the last three months on a condensed, accelerated reliving of the fourteen-year case that defined his reputation, yet tainted his life thereafter.

The case of Corbin Andrew Krell: Krell the Destroyer, Krell the Creator.

But Krell was incarcerated, buried deep in *The Pit* out at Stonewall, the maximum security prison, "on the border of Nevada and Hell." Vera had even made a trip there a month ago to verify that Krell still occupied his cell within those dark, dispiriting walls. As if the loss of hope mattered to Krell. Phone calls to the warden were not enough. He had to go there, had to see Krell in the flesh. Not a deed taken lightly.

Krell lived in his head constantly, even now. Fifteen months after his imprisonment, his philosophy and the video clips were a roll-call of torments Vera could never wash away. Only Vera's own death would silence the screams, the victims' surrenders, and Krell's soothing, soul-annihilating words.

When Vera had become a detective at twenty-seven, his motivation and spirit had been strong. He'd believed in justice, in right and wrong. Black and white. Rather patented and predictable and sounding like the spiel from some cigar chewing TV detective, yet he believed it to his core. He knew and understood there would be many sullied signposts along the way, showing him scenes and situations that measured darkness in blood and power, in minds gone to rot and obsessions mired in immorality. His resolve was stalwart. Even as he was put on the public map with his capture of Jimmy Nice, "The Bad Boy Murderer," and the messy finale to that one, his resolve remained solid.

Yet somehow— the job itself; the attrition of objectives; the heart of humanity gone black as a starless night— his stalwart resolve finally fractured, splintered, turned from oak to ash.

Humans catered to the whim of madness with an ease that battered him down, over and over again.

Krell, though, was pure evil, a step beyond madness. He was the reason Vera had lost his way. Over the years, after Krell had initiated his hellish objectives, there was nothing else *but* Krell.

He remembered Krell's words from clip number eight of twenty, victim number thirteen— Diana Bradley; Congresswoman Bradley from Oregon, a strong woman— as spoken in his reverberant monotone, as if somehow massaging words out of a steel plate.

"Evil is malevolent, feeding on depravity, humiliation, and perversion inspired by the corruption of self and soul. Evil dwells in the mental sewers that no man dare fully explore. Until me. Krell the Destroyer, Krell the Creator."

Vera's stomach roiled when he remembered what followed.

"Tell Detective Vera who you are." The words insinuated so much serene potency. They demanded the right response from Bradley. After a shockingly swift mental breakdown the camera focused on her make-up smeared countenance. Fiery pupils floated amidst puddles of deep blue eye shadow. Stray lines dripped off the edges of her cheekbones, cultivating an uneven, cubist digression worthy of Picasso. A bruise glowed neon red along her left cheek. Her bottom lip was split, smudged with blood, yet she smiled.

"Say your name...," Krell said, the voice of the snake,

the hiss as language, as influence.

Bradley's smile widened, ugly as a dropped watermelon as she said, "I am Honeyfuck."

Krell slapped her, a lightning strike from the right of the screen. The bruise flared, but the look on her face indicated she knew— *she knew*— it was deserved.

"Jesus," Vera's partner, Derek Sommers said, his voice smoldering with fury.

Vera watched in silence.

"Tell them who you are, *Honeyfuck*." The prompt from Krell's lips implied a depth of perversity Vera had never experienced, even with all he'd encountered with the job.

Bradley's eyes searched the room, settling on a point just beneath the camera. She started to salivate.

"I am...," she said.

A grunt of disapproval from Krell.

"I am Honeyfuck," she said— *in his voice, in Krell's voice*— a dark groan of defeat meshed with desire. "I am Honeyfuck, fuck, fuck, fuck," she said, pleaded, insisted, "This is who I am!"

Sommers turned from the screen in the small apartment Vera never called home anymore; it was only where he laid his weary head and empty heart. It hadn't been home since his wife, Marina, had left—

—*"You're barely here when you're here, Bobby," Marina said, ebony eyes for the man he used to be to somehow materialize again, sweep her off her feet and take her into his arms, his strength her home, their inhibitions not just discarded but never a part of the equation. Their passions unbound.*

"It's the job." A feeble excuse, the main excuse now, not even feigning the battle within to find other reasons to satisfy her. No longer willing to shovel shit as lies, the pungent stench of the truth was obvious enough.

"No, it's not just the job. You used to at least try. You would find precious moments with me. I lived for those precious moments. But it's been so long, Bobby, honey," she said, tears welling, her hand on his bicep. *"Ever since Krell..."*

Vera averted his preoccupied gaze from her, not wanting her to see the black rage that blossomed within.

"My heart wants to explode with the love I have for you, you know? ."

"Don't go." It was all he could muster.

"I'm sorry," she said. *"I don't want to, but I must. I can't live like this. I can't stand to see you like you are now. The man I love buried in a hell he may never climb out of. I love you so much, Bobby. So much."*

Vera watched Marina pick up her suitcase; she'd be back for the rest of her stuff later, when he was out, which was most of the time. Her long black hair glimmered in the uncertain twilight. He ached to run his fingers through it, to pull her close and taste her lips, her fire. She was the best part of him, his beacon through it all, the emotional tether he needed to balance the vagaries of the job, until Krell. Krell, a diseased thought, one he feared was a life sentence. He felt his heart would explode from anguish. He needed to say something, to stop this, but he knew there was nothing he could do or say that would hold any weight.

She turned to him, her softness a wish he might never envelop again. *"Call me if..."* Her voice wavered, yet she started again: *"Call me when you decide to be human again. I can't guarantee anything, but..."* She set the suitcase down and rapidly crossed the hardwood floor to him, the quickened pace of her footsteps matching the beat of his heart. She leaned up, slim fingers to his salt and pepper whiskered cheek, and kissed him. It was a precious moment, something to cherish. He inhaled the smell of *her: the crisp, lively spices that always danced off her fingertips and something not defined by lotions or perfumes, but distinctly her. Marina Vera nee Ojeda, a fervor ignited by the melding of the old soul animal within her and the firecracker steam and sensuality of the woman standing tall before him. She carried such strength, such wonder. What had he allowed to happen? Her aroma was a heady concoction that even now awakened every sense, suggested so many possibilities, destinations unknown taken without hesitation... yet they were not alone in his thoughts; never alone anymore. The bouquet was swift to fade as she hurriedly paced toward the suitcase and her exit, not looking back. She closed the door with a click that felt like a vacuum sucking the life out of him, if there was anything left to take.*

The hours into days into months since she left— almost two years now— were dotted with an occasional call from her, checking in, as if hoping to hear her Bobby again. Neither one of them filed for divorce, their marriage stuck in limbo. Missing her was a different type of torture. Often he would punch up her name on his cell and stare at it, unable to dial her number afraid of being sidetracked by the job that had overtaken his life; the job and, hence, Krell. He would set the phone on the table at the ready until the battery ran out, while in his head, all he heard was Krell's satisfied laughter—

—"I'm going to kill that bastard," Sommers said, striding with urgency toward the door. "Put a bullet in his head and fucking kill him."

"No, Derek. We won't sink to what he is. We won't..." But the words died as Vera watched Bradley move toward the camera, lowering herself as she did, a shaking movement rising up from below the screen. Krell stroked his engorged penis as Bradley took the scarred, swollen head into her mouth. Krell spit out the word, "No," and she reluctantly disengaged, her mouth still slack, her eyes mesmerized as Krell said, "Tell them again who you are." No hesitation from Bradley. Nothing but Krell's voice from her throat and Krell ejaculating in her face, ropes of semen slashing at her flesh— *singeing her flesh*. She seemed as though she wanted it, needed it. She repeated her name, her new name, over and over as it went on and on and gruesomely on.

Vera pulled his mind from the deep well of dread that Krell imbued into his every thought. He checked and rechecked the magazine in his Glock 21— a sleight of hand theft from evidence storage at the Oakland Police Department two weeks previous — sliding it in and out with practiced precision, though he'd only ever fired a gun three times outside of shooting ranges over the twenty-two years he'd been a detective.

Krell racked up a total of twenty-five victims over the span of fourteen years. He had murdered his first six victims, with his bare hands— strangling, pummeling— before adding rape to his repertoire, murdering and raping the next six victims. The following eight had been rapes, as the murders had ceased. There had been escalating degrees of mutilation, though. First from Krell, then, with the last three rape victims, by their own hands. These were captured on the video clips. The final five victims were not raped. Krell's evolving repertoire of horrors moved deeper into mutilation, specifically self-mutilation, in ways that stepped out of what Vera or Sommers or any of the FBI agents had ever imagined possible. He barely touched his victims beyond abduction, but it was his wishes they fulfilled.

The video clips started with victim number six. The thirteenth victim, the eighth video clip— Diana Bradley— was the first victim to live, if living was what one would call what followed for her.

Upon barging through the door to an apartment in the center of the city— a vacant though quite expensive rental— she had been found furiously masturbating in the bathroom, covered in her own filth as well as Krell's; even her hair was clotted with excrement. Sommers approached her as she moaned and cackled, calling her, "Congresswoman Bradley," which triggered her spitfire response as she slashed at him, fingers curled into claws, "I am Honeyfuck, you fuck. Honeyfuck, fuck, fuck you." She was feral, an animal guarding its kill: her soul... extinguished. Vera pulled Sommers away from her, away from the being who used to be Diana Bradley. Bradley was not even a memory within this new being's head. She was taken to an institution where, with no signs of change to this day, they medicate her just to make sure she does not rub her clitoris raw, her nipples and anus as well.

Sommers had eaten lead three months after Krell's capture as a means of escaping what he and Vera had experienced: touching base with true evil. Not some cut-and-paste Hollywood bastardization of evil. Not some worthy but failing fictional attempt at understanding true evil. Not some monster from the real world universally agreed upon as the embodiment of evil. No, true evil eradicated all previous conceptions of what it was. With Krell, it had moved beyond evil, though— this was the thing that Vera had gleaned over the years. Krell had evolved, more so, devolved, as it might be. Further evidence of Krell's transformation, no matter how unhinged the ambition seemed to Vera, was expressed in their recent, oblique meeting at *The Pit—*

—"Evil should not be, Detective Vera. Truly never can be. But in defining it as such, an inherent human bond with negativity confirms its very existence. Its mere

acknowledgement cancels its credibility. Evil is nothing— the lack of anything of substance— made concrete as a balance to everything else. Evil is not, yet it is a part of each human, because humans welcome its participation in their lives. They speak of it in anger or disgust, fear or even wonder— the most appropriate response— giving it a stronger foundation with every passing thought it distorts. Though within their pliable minds, they welcome it with the glee of the ignorant, nurturing the unthinkable, thinking the unimaginable, imagining the most horrid, abysmal designs, embellishing them with an insidious veracity until evil is as substantial a reality as their next breath. I strive for something else, beyond evil's claustrophobic clutches. I strive to transcend evil by becoming pure nothing. I strive as my followers strived." He paused, his ideology a cancer, spreading... "I am, yet I strive to not be. Do you understand, comrade?" His tone suggested fellowship, disciples of the same obscene religion. Vera did not believe evil and madness required mutual participation, yet with the latest developments from Krell in The Pit, he was not sure anymore. Because this latest stage moved beyond logic he could fathom. Krell hadn't even touched on the questions of his copycat follower, besides a curt, "My footsteps are deep. Many shall follow my path."

The room adjacent to the cell had reeked of a dense uncleanliness, a blackened suet of filth that coated walls and crawled as worms from Krell's gasping pores; part of a transformation only his company, his existence, could inspire. Krell remained in the shadows the whole time. When Vera had requested more light, Krell had said, "You won't want to do that," in a voice that vibrated through Vera's body. Everything about being in Krell's presence felt corrosive. When he left, bereft of any pertinent information besides the confirmation that Krell was indeed in Stonewall, in The Pit, he had vomited in the parking lot, purging a bit of Krell's poison from his system—

—Sommers' suicide note simply stated, "No more. Please. No more."

That was a year ago, only a year. Krell had been in The Pit for only fifteen months at this point. The more things change, the more they fucking stay the same, thought Vera. Then he spoke out loud, "No," his words pluming as mist in the frigid air as he checked the icy doorknob; it was unlocked.

He stepped inside and immediately headed in as direct a path as possible to an enclosed office to the far right, the only light in the building.

The copycat had to be there, the monster about to die, as Krell should have; as Sommers' fury had suggested.

Vera weaved between the dead shells of machinery gone to spoil. He sucked in dust but did not cough or sneeze. As he approached the wooden door, he could see the vague silhouette of a figure through the cracked glass to the right; a supervisor's office, watching over the ghosts, the decay.

He kicked at the door and stepped inside. Vera knew part of this he could not change would play out first, as before.

Stephanie Campbell, version two's victim number twenty-five, squirmed on the figure's lap, naked, more naked than any person he had seen since the first time he had witnessed self-mutilation of this mind-numbing enormity. She held a bloody scalpel in her left hand, having already dug deep ridges— some even to the bone— into her body; every inch of her body. Blood seeped moistly, congealing in clumps, glistening from everywhere. The stench made his eyes water. He didn't know how she still could be alive.

The new monster's voice cut through the buzzing in his head, as if a swarm of flies had taken roost in his skull.

"Tell Detective Vera *what* you are," it spoke, not as imposing as Krell's voice, but perhaps that was experience telling Vera it could not be; nothing could be. Yet it was so close, so close.

Vera cut in— "No— *stop*."— knowing it was a useless expenditure of energy, but something he could not help. What was the use anyway, what with Campbell's mentally, spiritually, and physically defeated condition?

The being that used to be Stephanie Campbell— a college professor, for God's sake; intelligent, opinionated— said in a voice much like this monster's voice, "I am... *Not!*"

Vera groaned out loud.

Campbell jammed the scalpel into her vagina and pulled up, scaling her torso, as if anxious to eviscerate herself, to show Vera, as the original victim number twenty-five— Alicia Amadae— had done, that she was *Not*.

Vera fumed in exasperation at the charade playing out before him, but there was no way to stop the inevitable. Campbell was already dead; it was simply the faint flicker of what once was that drove her onward with her final task.

The scalpel reached her sternum and she stopped and moaned as if in ecstasy. The new monster's large hands held her together from his perch behind her for a few seconds more as she repeated, "I am Not! I am Not! I am nothing! I am Not!" And he pulled her apart, her insides spilling out in stinking tides, blood gurgling from her mouth as well, her flesh husk and crumbling bones dropping into the pile of viscera that stained the concrete floor. Blunt and precise, as before.

That's when Vera saw the monster, naked as always, adorned in a smattering of scars, significantly less than Campbell's physical aberration, as if the copycat only dabbled and did not dive in, as his victims did. Vera thought it the one iota of Krell as human, too, perhaps a fear of pain, of suffering somehow derailing his intentions; the one suggestion of madness as opposed to the evil and now post-evil with which Krell draped his ideology. The sexual perversion was not a part of the pattern anymore, hadn't been for the last five victims. The copycat was simply naked, and rising up. That's when Vera scaled the new monster's body to take in its face— his face: Krell.

"Impossible," he said, as an Arctic exhalation passed through his body.

The copycat Krell laughed just as Krell had the first time, the sound of a muffler pitted with holes as it loomed over Campbell's steaming remains, as well as over Vera, not a small man himself. It was sadistic, and, as with Krell, indicated no soul buried within. Only a black hole of nothing, thought Vera— *you had succeeded you vicious fuck, can't you see?*— as he steadied himself and took aim at the large man, the monster wearing Krell's face.

Vera did not wait as Krell twin spewed, "Now the real misery begins, Detective Vera," instead, he wailed— the most appropriate enunciation of events having transpired— and squeezed the trigger again and again and again, until the whole magazine had been lodged into the new monster's head...

...and the copycat Krell did not flinch, did not speak. He seemed stunted as though the pattern were broken, but there was also something more that Vera could not gauge. He stared at Vera as Vera stared back, two who had obviously witnessed so much more than most humans could even imagine. Vera's gun-filled hand trembled as confusion laced knots in his forehead. His chest tightened.

He lowered the gun, his arm straining with the effort of wanting so much to destroy another human for what he had done to so many, but not understanding how a face full of lead had failed to do the trick. Not understanding anything as tears of frustration and impotent rage rimmed his eyes.

The new monster's face swirled oddly as white water rapids, as if the bullets were only a discomfort— nothing more— and the features regained the Halloween mask that was Krell's face.

"What's next?" he said, this new monster, the man like no other, not even Krell.

The voice circled Krell's with the intent of copying it, yet with the conclusion played out, he needed to use his own voice, his own words, which exacerbated its inflections. A copy, not the original. After all, how could anybody really follow Krell? Yet now, with this curious question.

Vera slumped to the concrete floor, exhausted. The knees of his black slacks were mere inches from Stephanie Campbell's pooling remains. He raised the emptied yet still hot barrel to his temple, pressed it there, and then dropped it down again. A perfect circle scorched his skin, a tracery of hair. Though he barely felt it, the corporeal remnants tinged his nostrils.

"You die," Vera said. "You have to die. You should be dead. That's what's next. How can this be?"

Krell's twin said again, "What's next?" in Krell's fading voice, as if the intonations were sculpted from uncertainty. It was the voice of the lost, the voice of a scared child.

Vera took this in, understood he was witness to something so out of the ordinary as to cast all he thought he understood about the grim world he lived into the wind.

He found the wherewithal to stand, regaining a semblance of composure. Frustration flushed from his system as bewilderment took hold and he asked, "What are you?"

The moment hung slack, and then stretched out, awaiting an answer. An answer like none Vera could have foreseen.

"I am nothing, in search of something. In search of... being. I... I and my others, fragments splintered off the deep shroud... out there." It turned its gaze upward, to the spider web-laden metal of the ceiling.

Vera understood it meant space, no matter its strange wording.

"We fled to the farthest reaches of... infinity. We are connected by... thoughts." The alien's mouth continued to move, but no words were spoken, as if it still did not have the full understanding of what to say. "We *hear* each other's thoughts. Our aim is to fit in. To... assimilate into the society of those whose planet we choose to... *be* on. To be. We find a random figure of the primary race of the planet we've chosen and follow it, learning the ways of the beings we wish to... live with. It takes time to get all the nuances... precise. From nothing to something takes time. I was still... still learning, when my mentor, the one I think of as Father Krell... never came back to his cabin not far from here. I had last seen him with the other one who had... opened herself. Watching from the shadows, as always, taking in the peculiar rituals of your kind, hearing Father Krell's laughter, before being called to my others during a time of need by one. This distraction pulled me... away. When I got back to the cabin not far from here, I waited. Father Krell never... never came back. I..."

Vera could see in its now soft, almost gentle eyes— the alien within peering out at him; alien, he thought: *alien*— the effort every word was for it, searching, hoping it found the right words to make sense.

"After a year of your time, in conference with my others, we decided the only way to get back in touch with Father Krell was... was to follow his every step, to draw his... attention. I was learning so well, but I needed to learn... more."

Dear God, *Dear God*, Vera thought, as he fully grasped the impossible confession of misguided allegiance to a monster made of flesh. Flabbergasted and light-headed, his legs turned to jelly as he stood in the desolate factory, listening to an alien being, perhaps the first ever to communicate with humans, tell him it had come to earth simply to fit in, to be one of us, and as a mentor, as a fucking father figure, it had stumbled upon Krell as an example of how we humans were. Krell the Destroyer, Krell the Creator; Krell, the human waste, the human monster. Not human at all.

Vera's shoulders sagged as he stared up at the alien wearing Krell's face.

The alien stared back at him and tilted its head with the wide-eyed curiosity of a newborn. Except for the mature nature of Krell's abhorrent undertaking, it seemed so young.

Everything simmered, the chill autumn still drawing wisps of dying heat from the inside out mess that was Stephanie Campbell.

"Krell... is a monster," Vera said.

"But he... he is human. He is like you, like—"

"Krell is nothing like me." Vera realized he would have to be specific. The alien, though able to copy what humans did, how we spoke— perhaps from television, perhaps only from Krell and his victims— really had no inherent understanding of what it was to be human, despite all the time with Krell; more so, because of all the wasted time with Krell.

Vera tapped the empty gun against his hip, thinking.

"Krell is the worst example of what it means to be human you could have found. There is right and wrong in this world. Good and bad." He thought black and white, but knew otherwise.

"What is right? What is wrong?" The inflections completely shifted away from Krell's. In finally using its voice, it was finding its own rhythm. Too late, after all that has come to pass, but perhaps with a chance to actually grow now. But how? Into what? He could not take the alien to prison. It wouldn't understand. It learned from the most despicable of teachers. Would it stay on earth, free to learn right, good, compassion, and love, as it would have if not for Krell? What exactly was next?

"Right is positive, the way of good," Vera said, and then stalled, turning to take in the warehouse, seeking answers in the deteriorating geometry. He wasn't good at this at all. Then it came to him, a different way, a path less clear but more understandable for the alien, he hoped.

"You have what you describe as a connection with your others, hearing thoughts..."

"To my best expression... to my best understanding of what I know of your language, yes. We are connected."

"Yes, that's it. Your kind, no matter trying to assimilate into different races, you are connected, working together for a common goal of understanding each race. That's what most humans try to do, work together for the common, well, good. Something positive."

"I still do not understand positive. Right. Wrong."

Vera shuffled slightly, knowing he was failing to make a dent, yet also knowing the alien was a sponge, and, somehow, with it put properly, would understand right, wrong, good, bad, and so much more.

"But you do understand connected, right? You are connected to those like you, as most people are connected, working for a common purpose."

"Yes, a common purpose. We exchange information. We communicate in our way and work toward a common purpose."

Vera holstered his gun, his fingers achy from the tension. He held up his right hand. "This... this is the majority of humans." He held up his left hand, with his thumb extended away from the rest of the fingers. "This is most humans... and this one finger, the thumb, is Krell." He moved his hands together, intertwining the fingers, except for the one indicated as Krell. "Most of us want to work as one, in unison, in a way that is good, right, and positive for all humans. Except for Krell." He wiggled the thumb.

The alien peered sharply at the thumb. Something registered, but Vera could not be sure, so he said, "Does that make sense? Krell is not a part of the rest of us. Krell is outside of most of our thinking, how most humans are." Simplification for the sake of teaching, as one would a child.

"Father Krell is not... one of you, of humans?"

No reason to defer from the bridge of understanding he was building between them. "No. He is a monster in human flesh."

"Krell is from out there"—signaling above again; space—"and not... here? Like me?"

"No. Not like you, either. He is human, but the worst kind. Wrong. Bad. Evil."

"This... right and wrong, good and bad, this is all there is to being human? Working together or not working together?"

"Not exactly, but they are major parts of the human puzzle," he said, knowing this really would make no sense to the alien. "I mean, there's more, there's more. Compassion and empathy: caring for other people, not destroying them, as Krell had done. Generosity and good will: giving of oneself in a way to others for the betterment of others, perhaps even the specific happiness of one person. Love..." He paused, realizing this was as much for himself as it was for the alien. "Love... when you find one human who matters more than all the others. The one you are connected to the deepest. The one who makes the most sense to you..." A tear trickled down the side of his nose.

"What is this?" the alien said, pointing to the tear. "So many of Father Krell's... of those who spent time with Father Krell did this."

Great, thought Vera. Now he had crossed even deeper

into the gray area.

"It is a tear. Often humans express their hurt, their sorrow and pain, with tears, but sometimes... sometimes it's more a longing, missing somebody. A different kind of hurt. Krell's victims were not crying— that's what it is called when we do this— out of longing, more so pain, hurt, the bad stuff. My tears are for missing the one I love."

"Missing the one you love? Is this a bad thing, too?"

Vera thought, I'm not a poet, I'm just a damned worn out detective. How am I supposed to explain tears, and love? Empathy and passion? "It can be, but it's different than that. I miss my wife, the one I am meant to be with. I miss her dearly. Love is the light within us all, and mine has been dim for too long. This ache... kind of lets me know I am still alive."

Vera dropped his head, stared at his shoes, knowing the sense of this was probably too much for the alien, when the alien said, "Why are you not with the one you love?"

Because I am a weak man. Because I am a pathetic man touched by evil. Because of Krell, the one who has destroyed what mattered most to me.

"Sometimes... sometimes the mere living is too much, and when you love somebody, you don't want to drag them down with you. I want to give her everything she needs, but circumstances out of my control have narrowed the path to her, made me perhaps wary of even trying."

Vera thought himself an inadequate teacher, an inadequate human, trying but failing to express some tiny scrap of what it means to be human.

What next?

"Does any of this make sense to you?" he said, failure a lunatic crow cawing outside the factory.

"No... Maybe. But from what you have told me, Father Krell has never... done... never expressed any of these things." The pupils within the alien's childlike gaze dilated.

Vera registered this as somehow good. Heart on its sleeve, better yet, understanding in its eyes.

Again, moments swelled unfilled, Vera sensing his efforts were for naught, when the alien said, "I think... I think I understand."

Vera wanted to smile, but the circumstances of where they were and what had happened there mere minutes ago, negated it; a nod of the head would have to do.

The alien's eyes seemed to come alive even more, as if it did really get it.

"Take me to Krell."

"What?" All feigned progress crashed and burned in Vera's mind. "Why would you want to see Krell?"

"Because... because he wants something I can give him."

The words sank as a lead weight clipped off the fishing line.

"Why would you want to give him anything? He's a monster. Didn't you understand anything I said? He's..." Then Vera saw in the alien's ever-transforming eyes: it knew exactly what it was saying. It understood on the simplest level, right and wrong. Good and bad. It knew exactly what it was suggesting. Now it was time for Vera to learn a thing or two.

"What do you mean that you can give Krell exactly what he wants?" Vera had to be sure.

"You know what he wants, Detective Vera," the alien said, its voice growing more firm— wet concrete, hardening.

"Yes, but... I want to know your interpretation."

"Interpretation?" Vera thought he'd lost the alien with a word out of its range, but the alien showed, with what must be its first ever conversation, that it was learning. "He wants to be nothing. I came from nothing. I have not succeeded in my quest to fit in and it's time for me to go back from where I came. I can grant him his ... wish. I can take him with me..."

"You can do that?" Vera said, astonished at the possibility: to be nothing as the alien understood it, nothing being its true father.

The alien quivered, its body melting and morphing from Krell's large, imposing figure, to the size of a short man, its features swimming as when the bullets struck its face, but, now different, almost human.

The hairs on Vera's body came alive, the transformation radiating as waves of static electricity.

The alien finally relaxed into a basic assimilation, one nobody would ever think out of place.

Vera took a faltering step backward, discomfort tingling on his skin, when the alien said, "Some of what is human is... ingrained in me. My pure self is... blank and cold and... nothing. This was as far as I had gotten in my assimilation. Expanding to a larger size, large as Father Krell or you is not all that... pleasing. I have... I had so much more to learn. But I've squandered my existence trying to be something that should not be. Talking to you... I feel I have learned more in... our time... than in all the time with Father Krell. I have learned more about what it truly means to be human. As for your previous question, yes, I can do that. I have... I understand enough of what you have... taught me to know it would be the... right thing to do. It's what I can give to you. It's what I can give to humanity. It's what I can give to Father"—pausing, cogs slipping into place— "to Krell."

Yes, the alien understood. What it would be doing in granting Krell his ideological quest in the crudest terms: the alien would be taking out the garbage.

He was definitely not a poet.

Vera moved around Stephanie Campbell's cooling remains and extended his hand toward the alien. The alien looked at it curiously.

"What's this?"

"It's my way of saying welcome to the human race. And thank you."

The alien extended its fingers and Vera gripped them, hard enough to leave an impression, but not hard enough to hurt. Vera smiled; the alien smiled back, wiggling its thumb before placing it in the grasp of the handshake.

"Connected for the greater good," the alien said.

A few hours later, in a small room adjacent to Krell's cell in The Pit, branching out as one of five dark corridors reserved for the worst of the worst, Vera and the alien sat, waiting. Vera had stopped by his apartment, an out of the way drive, but necessary to get the alien some clothes. He figured a pair of Marina's jeans and tennis shoes she'd left behind— left as a reminder of her, perhaps; as if he could ever forget her— and a too large white shirt and black blazer would have to do. I.D. for the alien would have to be Vera's word to Calvin Decker, the warden at Stonewall, a friend he knew would trust him when it came to Krell, even if they had different perspectives.

They sat in silence, not even the low hum of electricity daring to murmur here.

Vera had been to many prisons, been subject to the architecture of despair as constant companion. It was woven into the flesh of the guilty, an invisible straightjacket that clung to their every thought, as well as embedded into the walls, infused into the air. Despair was the cornerstone of the fetid ambience. Within prisons, life was not lived, it was endured. Each man's existence was defined by the terminal waiting. Trepidation kept the hackles on guard. No matter the warmth outside, the chill of dissolution snuggled into every cell, partner to misery, yet this was felt more intensely by an outsider than it was by those who walked the halls. The inmates bathed in this and let it wash over them, defiling perspectives and perceptions. Being ready for anything at any moment, finding pleasure in hollow couplings— willing or not— these were the things that drove them, that nudged them out of stiff cots and stiffer realities. Existence by rote, until a shiv or time or lethal injection or God squeezed the last breath out of them.

But down here, literally underground, the windowless realm of The Pit served notice to those of exceptional malice toward their fellow man, their days were numbered. Even calling them days was perfunctory. Time did not matter here. It roosted on a line strung taut between days, between the indistinct emptiness of one minute to the next. The illusion of day to night that turning the lights off for twelve hours, then on, ever dimly for twelve was a nod to denial, to not wanting to see him and what he did— manifests nothing but the lie of normalcy for those who did not cater to the basic precepts of normalcy, and most certainly did not bow to the best intentions of humanity, even as the world turned and grew more weary with every rotation.

The cold down here was subterranean, cave-like; of the grave.

For the guards already averting hard eyes and deaf ears from the lone camera watching Krell, the other senses curled up and hid within whenever they took him out for his one hour each day, or whenever food was delivered, or the pail for defecation was removed for cleaning, which had been useless for a few months now—

—*"He's eating his own feces, drinking his urine,"
Warden Decker said, a half hour earlier, the nonchalant
look on his face, a lie he liked to brandish.*

That might explain the stench, thought Vera.

"He's also eating the walls."

"What?"

*"This sick piece of shit is eating the walls," Decker said.
The thin, always dark skin beneath his right eye twitched.*

"How can he eat the walls?" The statement was the definition of surreal. Vera felt his heartbeat ratchet up a notch.

"You know how it goes in The Pit. He gets one hour in the yard per day, manacled and left to roam like a dog, that's it. While he's out, we spray down the walls of The Pit. That's when we noticed a large indentation on one side, little divots throughout. Sure, we got one camera in the corner, that's how we know of his other dietary habits. He must eat the walls when it's night, lights out, though..."

"Though what?" Vera's impatience simmered; Decker had always been one to meander when it came to relaying information.

"We only really see him well when he's on his walk in the yard. His mouth, his teeth, they're... different. His fingers, too. Then there's his constant monologue about what he's becoming. Or not becoming. His wish to be nothing. You know all that. He's a fucking cipher."

Of course he is, thought Vera. That was the gist of his aspirations. Vera knew it by heart, as did the alien standing silently next to him. This philosophy beyond good and evil, beyond reason and even madness haunted Vera's every thought. That's why Krell didn't qualify as simply a madman, as Decker believed, though Vera considered the possibility, especially with the developments since Krell had turned himself in. But for now, Krell remained something else, something more, and, apparently, changing—

—The heavy steel door opened. The light was again dim, purposefully so. Vera and the alien watched as two figures entered and moved to each side of the door. Krell followed, hunching down, his frame even more massive than Vera had remembered from only a month ago. Another guard followed, shutting the door.

"You know the drill," one of the guards said— hard to

distinguish which one, the direction of the voice unclear amidst the mutating shadows.

Krell sat down. The manacles on his legs fastened to locks jutting from the floor below him. On the table, he set his hands apart and the chain snapped into place on the iron table between them.

One of the guards coughed.

Vera's eyes burned. His nose hairs twitched in protest.

Krell's body stench and abhorrent breath reached out and touched him, slithered in and gnawed. He felt as if he would never be able to scrub it off.

Vera glanced at the alien. There was no sign it was disgusted by Krell's foul smell. There was sense in this, Vera knew, but he did not want to think on it. He had only one reason to be here again.

"Leave," Vera said to the guards.

"Excuse me, sir—"

"Decker knows. Just... leave."

The guards looked at each other and took Vera's word as law. It wouldn't take much to get them to ditch this loathsome creature's presence.

The cowl of shadows around Krell's head and torso remained thick, as if drawn to him. Vera was thankful for this. He could sense movement, heard the slight clink of metal as Krell got comfortable, or as comfortable as a man in his position could be. His huge, scarred hands rested as sleeping pythons on the table in clear view, the fingernails splintered, calluses thick along the tips, down to the first joint.

"Evil was such a feeble aspiration," Krell said, starting in as always. "Deeper into the well of anti-self. To be nothing, such a blissful existence. Or would that be anti-existence, friend Vera?" The shadows shifted around Krell's head, a suggestion of a smile.

"Never call me friend. We are not friends."

"Then what do I owe the pleasure of this meeting so soon after the previous one, *friend Vera?*" He was smiling now, for sure. Vera detested the cruel delight this monster got in torturing him, confirmed by his next statement: "We know I already occupy the dark spaces in your skull. I live in you, friend—"

"Stop!" This was too much. Krell's intentions siphoned the strength from Vera, his control whittled to nil. Krell might live in his head, might frolic there, but twisting the knife was not something Vera could handle. They both knew their connection; Vera simply wanted it cut off, amputated as a gangrenous limb.

"Allow me," the alien said, its tone akin to tenderness, and so out of place here.

"Who's your friend, friend Vera?"

Vera went to speak when the alien placed its hand on his wrist.

"No. You should probably go now, Detective Vera. There's nothing more for you here. Ever again. You need not... wonder..." The alien turned its head toward him, the transparent eyes letting him know it knew more than would seem possible: "You need not let his words harm you any longer."

"Who is this little fuck?" Krell said, leaning forward, his seething smile a distortion culled from torn lips and jagged teeth. Scabs filled the lower half of his face, some crusty, some oozing.

He was crazy and there was no denying it. His aspirations for evil were molded in the mind of a madman. Something about that smile, that horrid leer, signified to Vera that no matter the magnitude and undeniable focus— first toward evil, then toward not being— he simply was mad.

Vera pushed his chair back; the sound scratched harsh as rats in a barrel at his eardrums.

"What's going on, friend Vera? Who is this little fuck?" A sliver of unease tarnished Krell's features.

Waves undulated off the alien with violent force.

Vera stood and staggered backward; the chair toppled.

Krell pushed himself as far away from the table as possible, straining the chain, his fists clenched with the effort.

The alien discarded his tiny façade for the massive shell that was Krell; shell, within there was a being with more humanity than Krell had ever had.

At least Vera hoped so...

The transformative process relegated the clothing Vera had loaned the alien to an unraveled pile of thread awaiting the tailor's sewing needle.

"I am Krell... Father," the alien said, his voice calm. Not Krell's voice, his.

"How can..." Krell's resolute self-discipline, the concentrated menace he flaunted with glee, was haphazardly swept under the rug, lumped there as a dead body in his shape. "How...? Detective Vera, *what the fuck is going on?*"

He almost welcomed Krell's desperation after all these years. Vera would ordinarily bat thoughts of this nature away, but right now, in this room adjacent to a cell in The Pit, normal expectations were null and void, because a more profound awareness of the inconceivable held the reins.

"I am Krell, Father. Your fondest follower."

The chains kissed and clanked with enthusiasm as Krell struggled in vain to break free.

"Detective Vera—"

"I am going to give you what you want, Father Krell."

"What the fuck is that supposed to mean?" Then, again: "*Vera...*"

"You want to be nothing. My friend has the means to fulfill your heinous philosophical desires," Vera said, backing toward the door.

The alien turned to gaze at Vera. Buried in that horrible face, that nightmare façade— the face that had awakened Vera hundreds of times in a fevered mental agony— the gentle eyes revealed a peaceful elation.

"Thank you for what you have taught me, Detective Vera. Now, go." It turned back toward Krell.

Vera thought Krell might actually break the chains as the metal tore into the flesh of his wrists and backs of his hands.

"Your struggles are useless, Father Krell. I am here to grant you your one wish."

Vera knocked hard on the door. The guard opened it.

"I will make you nothing. I will... uncreate you."

Uncreate, thought Vera. *Uncreate.*

"Vera. *Vera,*" Krell wailed, his voice wrapped snug in fear's vice-like embrace.

The guard said, "Oh, my god," and crossed himself as Vera pushed him away and glanced back.

The alien leaned forward, arm extended toward Krell, palm outstretched. There was an instant when the shadows evacuated Krell's head, as if wary of what was to follow.

Vera's eyes met Krell's for the final time

No, Krell was not evil incarnate. He was a madman, evil at heart, but there were many of those prowling the dark corners and solitary hubs of this earth. He may have affected Vera deeply, but no more.

Lights flashed as swords during battle.

Vera shoved the door shut as Krell let out a yell of such deep, inconsolable shock, a depth never conceived. After all, Krell was only human, and being uncreated was not something any human had experienced before. As the alien had said, from nothing to something takes time. Vera expected from something to nothing would take time as well...

~

Hours later, his clothes discarded after a long, scorching shower to cleanse off what he'd been a participant in, and the years he'd been soiled by it, Roberto "Bobby" Vera sat at the kitchen table in the small apartment he did not call home, and poured two fingers of whiskey into the shot glass in front of him. He stared at it for a long time, and then nudged it away. He picked up his cell phone and scrolled to Marina's number. Tears welled and he did not fight them. Her name and number filled the screen, and his heart. His hands shook and he said, "No," to the memory of Krell forevermore.

"Why are you not with the one you love?"

Because I am a weak man. Because I am a pathetic man touched by evil. Because of Krell, the one who has destroyed what mattered most to me.

Not anymore.

He dropped his badge into the garbage can next to the table, without fanfare.

He wiped his eyes and held the phone in his now steady fingers. He stared at her name and number, the one who mattered more than all the others. The one whose connection ran deepest, to his soul. The one who, amidst the chaos of life in this often grim world, always reminded him what it meant to be human.

He stared, overwhelmed with joy and relief that the weight had been lifted, and pressed SEND.

Where the Light Won't Find You

Derek Jenner stomps toward the glass doors of the multiplex theater, though distinction as glass is negligible as they are adorned with posters for the movies playing as well as upcoming attractions. He pulls on one of the doors with a little more gusto than necessary; it swings out and almost hits a young woman wearing the ugliest pea green and black plaid jacket he's ever seen. She gives him a hard stare but says nothing. He smiles meekly— excuse me— as he holds the door open for her, but she chooses a less treacherous route and walks around him, entering through another door. As he steps into the massive lobby, he bumps into the lone cardboard standee floating in an ocean of green carpet. Iron Man tumbles to the ground, Robert Downey Jr.'s smirking face staring up at him as he leans over to pick it up and a wandering employee gives him the evil eye, as if he needs anymore bad luck today.

What he'd thought was anger is more so frustration and, after the thirty minute drive to the theater, it has pretty much dissipated as mist would beneath a rising sun. He can't even remember what petty, niggling event inspired it. He thinks about turning around and getting back to the apartment ASAP, to Daisy, to make up and perhaps get some afternoon delight, but knows how she is and how she'll carry the brunt of whatever they had argued about a little longer than she should, so since he is here, he might as well take in a flick.

Scanning the electronic movie board, nothing stands out. Though there is that new Arnold Schwarzenegger action flick, sure to be totally mindless nonsense, but right now that might not be a bad thing. Turning his brain off seems appropriate. Or turning around and heading to the studio for guitar practice— why waste the money here? But then, a title at the end flickers on and off before stabilizing, something called, *Where the Light Won't Find You*, and he's intrigued.

Walking to the ticket counter, Derek takes in the young woman adjusting her dark brown vest over her darker green uniform, adjusting her nametag as well— Emily— her long, straight, black hair shiny as pools of oil; shimmering colors mingle with the inherent sheen. Her lashes flutter, as she raises her eyes from her busywork. She breaks into a too large smile. This is obviously her first job. She's probably fresh out of high school.

Derek says, "Is *Where the Light Won't Find You* a horror flick?"

Emily's smile sinks as she skims over the register where, he assumes, the titles for the movies are listed, and she's about to say something when a small Asian man, Chinese, Derek thinks, slinks next to her and says, "That movie is sold out, sir." His voice is mellifluous, the accent light, though the statement is firm.

Derek glances around the sparsely filled theater, takes in an old couple haggling about something. The woman wearing the ugly pea green and black plaid jacket is buying popcorn, and a huge guy, football lineman huge, buys a few items from the concession stand, as well.

Emily says, "I don't see that one listed," to the old Chinese man, her complexion shading red as if she's confused or fearful. It's the look of a new employee who is worried about her job already.

The old Chinese man only says again, "That movie is

sold out, sir." The look in his eyes indicates he knows stuff,
deep knowledge, so what is he doing behind the counter at
a movie theater? He doesn't fit in here. He's dressed too
spiffy in a fancy midnight blue pinstripe suit, not even in
a uniform.

Derek harrumphs and leans back to peruse the movie
board. The Arnie flick starts five minutes after *Where the
Light Won't Find You*. The title for the latter seems to be
disappearing as he squints at it.

"What the hell. Gimme some Arnie."

The old Chinese man feigns approval, though his smile
seems more one of relief. He fades back, ambling to a corner where shadows hint at a doorway.

Emily smiles weakly, her anxiety obvious— she wears
it on her sleeve.

Derek laughs inside; just like his anger, frustration, or
sometimes brittle self-confidence. He hopes she can grow
out of it quicker than he. At twenty-eight, he still hasn't
grown out of it completely.

She says, "Ten-fifty."

He pulls a ten and a one out of his *Pulp Fiction* inspired
"Bad Mother Fucker" leather wallet and says, "Who was
that weird guy?" as he hands it to her.

Emily leans forward, conspiratorially, and says, "I don't
know. They don't tell me anything, I'm new here." Her
smile is blinding as she says this, back to her overly cheerful façade. "He showed up today by surprise and Bobby,
he's my boss, said he would just be hanging around and if
he makes any requests or anything, do as he says."

"Probably some corporate dweeb," Derek says.

She covers her mouth as she giggles— dear god, she
is young— and he remembers the last time he was in this
theater. A whole row of teenage girls sitting behind him
giggled and chatted and screamed their heads off at the
horror movie he saw that time. As Emily hands him the

ticket, change, and receipt, he wonders if she was one of them.

She says, "Number eleven, on your left."

The transaction complete, her glare-on-snow smile washes the previous few minutes' bewilderment from her recall.

He meanders over to the concession stand, a rarity for him as the prices are highway robbery, but he didn't have the wherewithal to grab a burger, fries, and a soda to sneak in under his jacket. Since today is winding down the road in a weird way, he figures, what the hell, and takes his place in line behind the mountain of a man, who has gathered enough food to feed a small army. He cups ice and root beer and has an employee get him a large popcorn. He pays and veers left to the hallway.

Walking swiftly, knowing he is cutting it close time-wise, Derek takes in the numbers and movie titles. Finally he finds number eleven with *Bad to the Bone* listed over the door, the new Arnie flick— a blatant nod to one of the most memorable scenes from the second Terminator movie. As he heads toward the theater, he notices the big guy entering a theater at the end of the hallway where he thought the men's restrooms were located. They must have recently remodeled.

Sold out? No way!

Let's see for sure. Derek hopes it isn't and is fairly sure it won't be. Screw the old Chinese bloke.

The sign, just like on the movie board, seems to lack the inspiration to stay lit. An undefined sense of urgency prods him as he practically jogs to the theater, popcorn leaving a bread-crumb trail behind him, a path back to safety. He smirks, not really caring about the mess, and pulls on the door handle. The door opens with a swoosh and he's met with a chilly breeze, an actual breeze that reminds him of a lonely walk along a harbor, not something whipped up by the movement of the door, and steps inside.

There is a moment where his head goes light. There is a moment where he thinks this all feels wrong. But both of these impressions are swept as dust under the rug and he strides along the wall to the front and glances up. The theater is empty except for him and the big guy, who already is at the back row, moving to the center, sitting down.

Friggin' asshole, he thinks, about the old Chinese man. Sold out? Friggin' asshole. Wonder what his problem is.

He nudges the second row seat and it's stiff, so he moves up to the third row and makes his way to the middle as well. He sits down and lets the smooth rocking motion of the chair take him into its comforting embrace.

He swings the arm rest down, sets the soda in the cup holder, grabs a handful of popcorn and stuffs his mouth. Closing his eyes, he thinks of Daisy. Why the hell do they do this to each other? So inane. They make so much sense together, except for these ridiculous diversions. He has a thought that it might be her period— once in a while she gets overly sensitive when it's kicking in— but knows better. It's more as if *he* is on his period, a sensation he gets every couple months when he is the overly sensitive one. He wonders if men get that kind of thing, too. Harrumphing to himself, he is already anxious to get home. He really loves this woman.

That's when it strikes him there is no music, no nothing. The place is dimly lit, as expected, but there is no pre-movie bullshit.

The lights dim. The movie commences. No trailers; no nothing. Par for the strange course, he thinks, as he settles in.

The screen is completely black. So black it seems to be draining any excess light from the theater. The title vacillates in the blackness, much as it had done outside. That is it for opening credits as he is taken into a car with some teenagers heading out to the woods. After a few minutes of dull dialogue, they spot a cabin. He almost groans out loud, catching himself before making his displeasure so obvious. Sure, he might be one of only two people in the theater, but he doesn't want to annoy the other patron, that isn't his nature. Not like those giggling teenage girls from the last movie. He understands movie etiquette. As if there is such a thing nowadays, he thinks, before his thoughts weave back to his heart, and Daisy. Man, this would be so much better with her here.

The movie moseys along. All the cliché pieces slot into place as if by rote. He finishes his soda and most of the popcorn in the first half hour. At that point, the seat behind him squeaks. Yeah, big guy, he thinks, it is that bad. Maybe he's getting more food— no way!

Another seat squeaks closer behind him. Derek turns. The big guy has moved up about halfway. He does a weird, beauty-pageant-winner-in-a-parade stiff fingered wave, quite unnerving— Mr. American Asswipe, circa two-thousand... whenever.

Derek turns back to the movie. The big guy in the back makes him feel more uneasy than anything from this dud of a flick.

After another half hour or so, the movie gets a little creepier. The characters are all trapped in a small cellar— standard Stephen King protocol— and something supernatural is messing with their minds, creating hallucinations of hideous design.

A seat squeaks behind Derek. The sound makes him jump. It feels as though a fingernail of dread *click, click, clicks* down his vertebrae. He also senses the cold breeze again, a beached whale's death exhalation. The combination of the movie amping up and the trepidation from the seat creaking makes him clench his jaw.

Heavy footsteps pad toward him from his right. The

fingernail of dread becomes a full handful and plays a macabre drum solo up and down his spine.

The big guy slowly lumbers down aisle four and sits directly behind him.

Derek doesn't even turn around to check. His nostrils are assailed by the smell of the rarely showered poorly concealed by stale cologne. The smell of something else, too, something fishy underneath, which makes sense, what with the initial smells upon entering the theater reminding him of a pier. The big guy must work at the boardwalk.

Derek scrunches down a bit, then thinks, what the hell am I doing? He sits up tall. Screw this! Screw all of this. This big guy might be a mountain, but there's a whole god-damned theater here and he's decided the best seat in the house is right behind me?

Derek's ready to turn and give the big guy an earful, but his fragile confidence is never this brash. Instead, he finds himself sinking down into the seat again; his composure frayed as cat-scratched curtains.

He tries to focus on the movie and not think about the guy behind him. After a couple minutes tamping down his agitation, he coughs and hears a tiny snicker echo in response. He catches his breath and again tries to focus on the movie.

On the screen, the guy with the professionally tousled, brown hair and the too perfectly trimmed twenty-four hour shadow is reading with a flashlight the last lines from something scribbled on the wall in too-runny movie blood. The plucky blonde who has uncharacteristically— for a horror flick of this meager ilk— not removed her skimpy baby doll tee hangs on his arm and every word.

He says, "The dread is in knowing you will have to for-ever live where the light won't find you." The flashlight goes out.

The screen goes dark. Too dark.

After twenty seconds or so— twenty seconds that feel like twenty minutes to Derek— there's a thump on the back of his seat. His heartbeat picks up its pace, attaining a strong gallop.

Another ten, perhaps fifteen seconds pass before the big guy sitting behind Derek, that mountain of a jerk, makes some hacking, gurgling sounds, as if he is pulling up a mouthful and is planning to decorate the back of Derek's head with the green slime.

The silence heightens these strange, throaty sounds.

Seconds tick by; soldiers on a mission.

Then, the friggin' jerk kicks the back of Derek's seat. Tap, tap, tapping, as if those soldiers have picked up the pace to a jog, trying to catch up to Derek's rapid fire, double-bass drum heartbeat.

Derek shoots straight up from his seat, turns to say something, anything, to this major fuckwad, no matter he is big as Godzilla, when he sees what is really responsible for the sounds.

Perched on the big man's chest is a glimmering creature with a proboscis jammed into the top of his head and dozens of spindly, multi-jointed limbs still thwacking Derek's seat. Shock flushes adrenaline through his whole system. Any vocal reaction is traffic jammed in his throat. His brain reels as he shuffles back the few inches he can.

This creature that might be an insect but isn't, though the mechanics scream insect, looks to be feeding on the big guy.

The man's eyes are wide open and despite the darkness, the mottled, off-white skin of the thing— it is more skin than exoskeleton, alien, obscene— is luminous.

On the back of the creature, or what he presumes is the back— there are no certainties here— bulbous, jelly-like surfaces quiver. Images flash on the membrane. Murder, torture, rape. This is a horror movie to obliterate all other horror movies. Since the scenes star the big man, Derek interprets them as snippets of the horrors he has doled out in his life. He clenches his fists, wanting to batter the big man and stop the torments and alleviate the broken masks of pain distorting the faces of the victims, but the action would be superfluous, as they've already transpired. There is nothing to alleviate anymore. And this is no time to be rubbernecking.

He tries to turn. His legs won't move — paralyzed.

The big man gurgles, his plea made concrete, "Help me." The words are sloppy, wet as a slaughtered cow still shuddering on a concrete killing floor.

"I warned you away from this movie, Mr. Jenner."

Startled, Derek follows the voice to the figure standing directly to his right, already stepping into the row, approaching him. The old Chinese man.

"What the hell is going on? How do you know my name?"

"My name is Mr. Liu." He extends his hand.

Derek shrinks away, his feet stutter-sliding along the sticky theater floor, finally able to move. He hasn't made a new friend. He isn't going to agree on a deal. He wants nothing to do with any of this.

"Fine, Mr. Jenner." Mr. Liu pats down his exquisite midnight blue pinstripe suit. The light from the creature sparkles on the radiant fabric. "You were warned away from this movie for a reason. Mr. Blaylock here has exceeded his usefulness on this planet. He misused his power, his purpose."

"Purpose?" The polished glimmer of one of those big knifes used at the piers for gutting fish plunges repeatedly into an old man's chest, his throat, an eye. Blood geysers as the big man continues to thrust and thrust and thrust, his expression one of bliss. "This is his life playing out, right? These are his murders and shit playing out, right? He's a damned murderer, right?"

"Correct, Mr. Jenner. You are perceptive, but not smart. You should have—"

"What line has he crossed besides murder? What godforsaken purpose did he have that would be deemed useful?"

"Yes, he is a murderer." Mr. Liu steps closer to Derek. Derek instinctively steps away. "But there's more to him than that."

"What usefulness, then?" Derek is again surprised he's asking questions, but he's buying time. He senses his survival instinct flailing. *What the hell has he gotten himself into?*

A row of what Derek takes to be eyes rotates within the malleable flesh to the back of what he thinks of as the creature's head and settles on him. They are not exactly eye-shaped, more like stars with blunted points. The glossy white centers dilate as they take him in. A spasm ripples over the creature's body, as if it has just realized Derek is watching it. A stentorian rumble emanating from who knows where makes the hairs on Derek's arms not only stand at attention, but brace for the worst.

The desire to back away fizzles to ash in the hearth of his hope: there is nowhere to move. To his right, Mr. Liu blocks his escape. He could shove him aside with ease, but what of the consequences? To his left, huddled in the shadows more strangely shaped figures fill the darkness. An unknown light source trims their abysmal silhouettes like stained auras, treating Derek to their warped presence. Acid stirs in the cauldron of his stomach.

Something hisses and sizzles.

An utterance, like what melting wax would sound like if it had a voice, hovers above him. No, there is no escaping this predicament.

"You warned me, okay. I... I understand this much. But what now? Can I go?" His survival instinct ratchets up, though it is tenuous at best, greased and slipping through his fingers with every passing second. "I need to leave, man. I don't belong here—"

Another strange sound, like feverishly flapping moth wings made from tinfoil draws his head to the side. The joints in his neck crack. He tries to shake the sound from his ears but it burrows deeper inside...

Then at the end of the row, a kaleidoscopic array of brilliant colors pulses from within a floating square-shaped thing about the size of a basketball.

It moves slowly toward him.

Mr. Liu turns to it. The thing's pulsing intensifies. The sounds prickle spastically, playing a disjointed jazzy rhythm. Derek hates jazz.

Mr. Liu turns to him and says, "I'm afraid you've made a mistake, Mr. Jenner. You were warned to avoid this movie." Mr. Liu peers over his shoulder for seconds that slosh through mud, the slow trek a Chinese Water Torture to his hope. "There was business to attend to that no human should witness. My employers deal in keeping balance amidst the chaos of the universe."

"Balance? How does this relate to... him?" Derek says. The creature pulls its sword-like proboscis from the big man's head. With twitchy movements the pointed tips of its many limbs pluck pieces of fabric and flesh. Apparently, it is still hungry, still eating.

"We are a volatile race, Mr. Jenner." He opens his palms in an all-inclusive manner— the universal "we"—as if Derek feels any kinship to this strange man. "When humanity is in danger of becoming lost, my employers must make adjustments to keep the balance. Mr. Blaylock's penchant for killing was in its way part of a justified balance."

Derek cringes at the thought that murder could be essential for "justified balance."

"But recently he has undertaken deeds of a more dire

malevolence, rendering his usefulness obsolete. He had a purpose, but now, as you've put it, he has crossed the line."

The square-shaped thing chatters ever louder at Mr. Liu, perhaps tired of waiting for its meal: Derek. Or perhaps it has something else in mind, something he hasn't the imagination to summon. This situation annihilates the boundaries of anything he has ever experienced.

"I made a mistake. I entered the wrong movie. It was a mistake, I admit that," Derek says, as much to the square-shaped thing, whose colors have congealed into a singular hot pink accentuated by wisps of smoke that shimmy off its body, as to Mr. Liu. "I don't deserve this, any of this—"

"Mr. Jenner." Mr. Liu exhales sharply. "It's out of my hands." He steps back to let the square-shaped thing pass.

The smell of burning flowers, boiling lemons and foreign odors he cannot categorize clogs Derek's nostrils.

"Wait," he says, holding up his hand. The heat from the square-shaped thing makes his fingers bend backward in ways impossible for bones to bend, yet it does not hurt. He yanks his hand back. The fingers bend back to normal, but at least the action has caused the creature to stop its approach.

Unsettling sounds ricochet off the walls.

"Wait!"

What words to say? What words to wield?

"I made a mistake. I'm not part of this situation as it was supposed to play out. Don't you think letting me go makes more sense... in keeping the balance of the earth, the universe. Won't taking my life tip things?" Derek punches through his fright with reason.

Mr. Liu swats away the reason. "No, your death would not mean anything to the balance of the world."

Derek sags, sensing defeat.

"You are a minor player. Some would mourn. But you are not crossing lines, as was Mr. Blaylock."

Derek considers his insignificance. His loss really won't matter too much to anybody. His mom and two sisters, a few friends— Daisy.

Daisy and their love. How much does that matter? It does matter. Together they matter. In spite of the outrageous situation he has gotten himself into, they do matter.

"Since my life doesn't make a difference either way, let me go and I promise I will never speak of this, never tell a soul of what I have witnessed." Derek feels as if he is bargaining against the house, a stacked deck, fixed dice.

Mr. Liu raises an eyebrow, a white crescent as the moon winking. He turns to the square-shaped thing. A cacophony arises. The tinfoil moth wings flap wildly.

Derek experiences it not only aurally, but in his bones, his muscles, his thoughts; in every quivering molecule, in every atavistic aspiration or futile delusion of being. The sound fully engulfs him as neurotransmitters frantically crackle and spark within him, yet he stands his ground, watching as Mr. Liu, making no sounds, somehow converses with this thing.

A minute passes, two, three. Much longer and sounds will break Derek into tiny pieces, much as a baseball shatters a window.

The sound is abruptly clipped off. The sudden vacuum of silence, like a jolt of electricity, forces him to stand tall, regain his posture of faux courage.

Mr. Liu wipes his hands on his slacks, and then rubs them together, not with mad scientist glee, but with a sense of satisfaction. "They never have been subjected to an intrusion before. They find your desperation fascinating. Not all creatures in the universe understand the restrictions of life and death as we humans do; not all creatures cater to the limitations we believe we are ruled by. I've elucidated these facts to my employers, and negotiated with them on your behalf, Mr. Jenner."

He has a chance. He might get out of this alive.

"They will grant you your freedom, but you must promise you will never speak of what you have witnessed, of any of this. Ever." Mr. Liu swipes the empty space with his hand, as if shoving away the possibility of failure. "At the first hint of this, they will take you, Mr. Jenner. They may seem monstrous to our human understanding, but they are not. They are simply caretakers of the universe."

Derek thinks of the big man, and his grim fate. The monster draining him of every essence of his being.

"You should celebrate the magnitude of what they are risking by granting you your freedom. But since you were never supposed to be a part of this, they are showing restraint and even faith that you will keep your word." Mr. Liu approaches Derek. This time, Derek stands firm. "They need balance, certainty. As I've said, in your case the balance involves you remaining silent about what you have seen, what you have experienced, forever. It may seem a simple task, but you know how we humans can be, don't you?"

Without reservation Derek knows— to his core, to his soul— he will never speak of this to anybody. This is his burden to carry. It seems simple, but he even with his often fractured emotional base understand the pitfalls of being human.

Mr. Liu raises his small, aged hands toward Derek's face.

Derek is inclined to flinch, but knows Mr. Liu means no harm.

Mr. Liu pulls Derek's face down to his lips and kisses him on the cheek.

An icy chill burns Derek's cheek and he brings his fingers up to rub it. The sensation fades, though he senses it still lives there, whatever it is.

Whatever it is, it is now a part of him.

"When you are getting too close, the frozen fire will burn your cheek. That will be a warning, Mr. Jenner. Heed it without reservations. I hope you will succeed." Mr. Liu squeezes Derek's bicep, his voice a heart-to-heart murmur. "Believe me when I say, you do not want to fail."

Derek stares into Mr. Liu's intense, yet now somber eyes, acknowledging the inflexible truth of the statement. He must never cross the line, never think it safe. Never speak of them.

"Please, Mr. Jenner. I don't ever want to meet you again. The circumstances would be... less than cordial." He falls silent and turns away, walking briskly down the row.

The square-shaped thing is gone. Derek hadn't noticed it leaving. The big man and the monster that fed on him, the hunched over, spindly-topped figures in the shadows, are also gone. He glances right and left and back to where Mr. Liu should be walking down the stairs and he is gone as well.

"Mr. Liu?" Derek says— a cracked sidewalk whisper. The darkness is oppressive. He hastily strides down the aisle, descends the stairs, and steps into the lobby.

He moans in anguish: dusk tints the empty lobby. It is impossibly empty; no employees man their stations. How can it be so late?

Derek runs toward the doors. The glass between the posters shows him the desolate view outside. There are buildings and cars in the parking lot, but no people. His world does not feel like his world. *Mr. Liu, I thought we made a deal.*

"Mr. Liu," Derek says, imploring, "You said I would get my" —pushing the door open, the midday sunlight bathes him, blinding him, the heat and people and life bristling and alive all around him— "freedom."

His legs wobbly, he practically drops to his knees to kiss the concrete, when he hears a voice say, "I knew you'd be here, asshole," not in a way that expresses hostility, but affection.

Daisy, cigarette in tow, leans against the theater wall. She wears snug jeans and a White Zombie T-shirt. Her dyed, blood-red hair is pulled back into a loose pony tail as if she's just tossed herself together.

As Derek wipes moisture from his tear-stained face, her look shifts from playful to concerned.

"Hey, baby, what's wrong? She crosses the ground between them. "Hey..." she says, wiping his tears. Her warm hands feeling strong and soothing on his cheeks. "Hey, Derek, honey..."

"I'm fine, I'm fine..." he says, breaking into a big grin.

"What's with the tears?" Her tone seems genuinely worried.

"I'm fine, really, just..." But what can he say? Nothing is his only choice. Heat singes his cheek from within, one final reminder.

Never, he thinks. Never.

"If you say so," she says. She takes his hand and snuggles close to him, pressing in hard.

"Tell me you didn't waste our hard-earned money on the new Arnie cinematic turd, did you?"

"Yes," he laughs; yes, yes, that will be the story.

"Oh, my god, you are such a dingbat," she says, joining in his laughter. "He's just a shoot-'em-up joke at this point. And a cheating prick, too!" She pauses and tries again. "So, what was with the tears, Derek? You can't tell me Arnie's inept exploits made you cry."

"Just something in my eye," he says, glancing back at the marquee. There was no sign of *Where the Dark Won't Find You*. "Just dust or something..."

"I better be the only thing in your eye, lover boy," she says, squeezing his hand and rising up on her toes to kiss him on the cheek.

The same cheek.

Her lips feel soft and lightly wet. The sensation now not one to inspire trepidation, only elation. Like heaven. Yeah, I can deal with this. I may be insignificant in the whole of this harsh, strange universe, but I can deal with this just fine.

He grabs her ass and she squeals. He can't wait to get home, to love her right.

~

As Mr. Liu watches them leave, he senses perhaps Mr. Jenner will succeed and this will be the last time he will ever see him. This thought brings rare comfort to him. Something he appreciates.

The day's events were inconsequential— *something insignificant*— but in the scope of the bleak eternity that stretches before him, they are something to cherish.

Acknowledgments

Thank you to Jason Duke for invaluable feedback, and to Kate Jonez for her keen editorial eye. She helped make these tales sing. And to you my readers, who make this all worthwhile.

About the Author

John Claude Smith originally wanted to be a horror writer; now he's not sure what it is he writes, he just knows it is dark, and he's the one holding a flashlight, shining light on those places most people would want to avoid, scribbling notes.

He has written fiction, poetry and bad lyrics for as long as he can remember. At a point when he decided to get serious with fiction, sending out stories and getting a few acceptances in the early 1990s, he was side-tracked for many years by music journalism (as JC Smith), including stints as the industrial, experimental, gothic, metal, and all fringe categories reviewer for a variety of magazines including *Outburn, Industrial Nation, Side-Line*, and *Alternative Press*. He believes the over 1,100 reviews, articles, profiles, etc., he wrote helped hone his skills for the fiction gig. Finally back on the fiction path, he's had over 60 short stories and 15 poems published, as well as a debut collection of "not your average horror," *The Dark Is Light Enough For Me*. He is presently writing his third novel, while shopping around the other two. Busy is good.

He splits his time between the East Bay of Northern California, across from San Francisco, and Rome, Italy, where his heart resides always.

20365614R00076

Made in the USA
Middletown, DE
23 May 2015